BOX OF TRICKS

By Ellie Boswell

THE WITCH OF TURLINGHAM ACADEMY

UNDERCOVER MAGIC

SECRETS AND SORCERY

BOX OF TRICKS

THE WITCH OF TURLINGHAM ACADEMY

BOX OF TRICKS

ELLIE BOSWELL

LITTLE, BROWN BOOKS FOR YOUNG READERS
lbkids.co.uk

LITTLE, BROWN BOOKS FOR YOUNG READERS

First published in Great Britain in 2013 by Little, Brown Books for Young Readers

A CIP catalogue record for this book
is available from the British Library.

ISBN 978-0-349-00146-3

Typeset in Minion by M Rules
Printed and bound in Great Britain by
Clays Ltd, St Ives plc

Papers used by LBYR are from well-managed forests
and other responsible sources.

MIX
Paper from
responsible sources
FSC
www.fsc.org
FSC® C104740

Little, Brown Books for Young Readers
An imprint of
Little, Brown Book Group
100 Victoria Embankment
London EC4Y 0DY

An Hachette UK Company
www.hachette.co.uk

www.lbkids.co.uk

With special thanks to
Leila Rasheed

ONE

Sophie pushed through the crowd gathered in the grounds of Turlingham Academy and stood on tiptoe to see over someone's shoulder. All the pupils, reporters and visitors were outside to watch the big event. Today the teachers of Turlingham Academy were digging up the time capsule, buried when the school was first built. Sophie couldn't wait to see inside – it was 300 years old!

The boys' headmaster, Mr Pearce, and the History teacher, Mr McGowan, were digging away just

ELLIE BOSWELL

inside the fence. They both looked hot and red-faced.

Sophie heard her mum's voice and craned to see her talking to a local reporter. 'We discovered its existence as we were researching for a book about the school's history,' she said. 'Turlingham has a quite extraordinary library ...'

Sophie felt a hand on her shoulder. 'Hey, Sophie!' It was Katy. And she was holding hands with Callum. 'Extraordinary library is right, right?' she said, her green eyes sparkling.

Sophie grinned; she and Katy had had incredible adventures in the library. Sophie's mum might be the headmistress, but even *she* hadn't known about the real secret at Turlingham until a few weeks ago. There was so much more than a time capsule here: there was a magic library underground, full of spell books and magical booby traps!

Sophie hugged her friends hello, then stood back and put her head on one side to look at them. 'I know it's cold, but do you have to hang on to each other's hands quite so tightly?' she teased.

Katy and Callum turned matching shades of red. But they didn't drop their hands. Sophie was glad they'd finally got together.

'It *is* cold,' Callum said. He leaned in to whisper to Sophie. 'Hey, Sophie, can't you do something about the temperature?'

Sophie shivered, but laughed. She could hear waves pounding on the cliff below the lighthouse and the wind blustered around her ears. She looked up at the lantern room at the top of the lighthouse, where the beacon was. That was where she'd cast her very first spell, only a few months ago.

'You've got used to the idea of me being a witch pretty fast!' she whispered back. Callum was her oldest friend, and it had been really horrible having to keep her magic secret from him. She still couldn't tell most people – there were too many witch hunters on the prowl, searching for witches like her to demagick, or even kill. But Callum would never betray her to the witch hunters.

Not that all witch hunters are bad, of course. She smiled at Katy. *In fact, one of them is my BFF!*

'Give me your gloves,' she told Callum. She took

them and rubbed them together in her own gloved hands. 'Earth, water, wind and fire,' she whispered. 'Great forces of the Earth, make these gloves doubly, triply, um ... quadrupedly warm!'

The crescent-moon ring she wore beneath her glove tingled as magic flowed through it. Then she handed the gloves back to Callum.

'Wow, toasty! Thanks, Soph.' He pulled them on, then hurriedly took Katy's hand again. 'Better hold hands anyway, just in case,' he mumbled.

Sophie laughed; magic was no substitute for love!

'Guys!' A loud American voice cut through the crowd. Sophie looked up to see Erin grinning as she hurried towards them, pulling her boyfriend Mark along behind her. After them came Kaz with her boyfriend, Oliver, and then Lauren and Joanna.

'This is so awesome!' Erin jumped up and down in excitement, her blond plait jiggling. 'A three-hundred-year-old time capsule! That's like, older than the USA. Um – I think.' She frowned and began counting on her fingers.

'Yeah, who would have thought that Mr McGowan's

research would actually have turned up something interesting?' Kaz agreed.

'I can't wait to find out what's in it.' Little Lauren rubbed her freckled nose, which was pink with cold. 'Maybe it'll be worth millions.'

Erin's eyes lit up. 'Gold bracelets ... necklaces ... rings ... what could be cooler?'

'I'll tell you what's cooler – the anniversary party!' Kaz said, and everyone agreed loudly. 'Have you heard anything about it from your mum, Sophie?'

Sophie nodded. 'It's going to be huge! They'll be displaying the contents of the time capsule at the party. And there's going to be a school concert with everyone involved.'

'Great!' Joanna clapped her hands. 'I've been practising my violin.'

'They're going to invite parents and people from the village too,' Sophie continued.

'I was thinking of getting a band together,' said Oliver. 'Do you think we could perform?' He mimed air guitar and Kaz joined in.

Sophie opened her mouth to reply that she thought

so, but at that moment there was a loud clang and Mr Pearce shouted out, 'I've hit something! I think we've found the time capsule!'

There was a murmur of excitement from the crowd and everyone surged forward. In the confusion, Sophie was pushed to one side, and stumbled. Someone grabbed her arm and saved her from going over.

'Thanks!' she gasped. She caught her balance and turned round to see who had caught her. 'I almost fell head over ...' She tailed off as she found herself looking into a familiar face – Ashton Gibson, Katy's brother, was holding her arm.

'Are you OK?' he asked.

Sophie was speechless for a moment, and not just because of his gorgeous deep green eyes. It was the first time she'd seen him since he had asked her out, and she had said no.

She gave him a shy smile. 'Yes, I'm fine. Thank you.'

He let go of her arm and stepped back. She could see the disappointment on his face as he said, 'Sorry. I didn't mean to ... I'll go now. I know you can't stand me.'

Sophie felt sorry for him as he turned away – at least, that's what she *thought* she felt. When it came to Ashton, sometimes Sophie didn't know what to think. He was a witch hunter, and she was a witch. He'd been horrible to her when he first arrived ... but he said he was going to change.

'Wait,' she said quickly. She reached out and touched his arm. 'Don't go. I'd like us to be friends. If you want to.'

He turned back. 'I'd like that.'

Sophie twisted her gloves in her hands as Ashton walked away. He looked so sad that she wished she could run after him and give him a hug. Maybe there was more to him than she'd thought ...

But no. She couldn't forgive him for being so horrible to her and Katy.

She hurried after her friends and caught up with them at the edge of the hole.

'Stand back, kids,' Mr Pearce was saying. He and Mr McGowan wrestled to pull something out of the ground. It shone bright in the winter light: an iron box, secured with a heavy clasp.

Everyone around Sophie sucked in their breath.

Mr McGowan lifted the box up so everyone could see it. His face was red and sweaty but delighted. 'Ladies and gentlemen, boys and girls of Turlingham Academy! Here it is – the time capsule buried in 1713 by the first Master of Turlingham.' He put the box on the ground. 'This is a great moment in history; as we shake hands across centuries with our predecessors. Who would have thought that back in the 1700s, when as we all know the Enlightenment was flourishing not only in Europe but—'

'Just open it already!' called Erin.

Sophie giggled and even some of the teachers laughed.

'You're quite right,' said Mr McGowan. 'This isn't a History lesson, this is history in action!'

He tried to undo the metal clasp but it didn't move.

'Ah … it seems to be stuck. Not surprising, of course, it's been buried for so long.' He shifted his grip on the box and tried again. Sophie watched with everyone else as he fumbled.

'May I help?' Mr Pearce moved forward. 'It seems quite simple, there's a pin here … '

Together, the teachers struggled with the box, their smiles slowly fading. The crowd had fallen silent now and the sun seemed to have gone in.

'Why won't it come open?' Lauren murmured.

'Why are we wai-ting . . .' Kaz sang under her breath. Sophie giggled.

Sophie's mum stepped forward with an embarrassed laugh and addressed the crowd. 'So sorry for the delay. I'm sure they'll have it any minute now.'

'Let me try.' Mrs Freeman, the girls' housemistress, strode forwards and aimed the blade of her shovel directly at the clasp of the box.

'What are you doing? That's an ancient artefact!' Mr McGowan leapt forward, but he was too late to stop her. The shovel hit the clasp. Sophie winced, expecting the shovel to shear through the metal. But instead there was a clang and the blade bounced off.

Sophie looked at the box. It didn't have a mark on it.

'Wow! It's bulletproof,' said Erin in astonishment.

'That's so rubbish,' Kaz moaned, and everyone nearby echoed her.

'What's the point of a time capsule you can't open?' said Lauren.

Callum frowned and opened his mouth as if to speak, then seemed to have second thoughts.

'I must apologise,' Sophie's mum said, looking embarrassed. 'It looks as if it doesn't want to open. But not to worry! We'll work on it, and we'll have the contents on display at our anniversary party.'

There was some polite applause, but Sophie could still hear disappointed muttering. The crowd broke up, the visitors heading for the big iron gates, the students drifting back towards the school. It loomed up like a great grey cliff, all turrets, spires and gables, with seagulls surfing on the wind overhead.

Sophie was left alone with Katy and Callum.

'Well, that was a bit of an anti-climax,' she said, shrugging at her friends, expecting them to agree. But they didn't. They were both pulling the exact same face – frowning and biting their lips.

'What?' she asked.

Callum and Katy looked at each other, then at her.

'Don't you think it's strange,' said Callum, 'that an

iron box, buried in mud for three hundred years, hasn't got a bit of rust?'

Sophie thought about it for a second. 'You're right,' she said. 'And it's not like it was covered in plastic or anything. How weird!'

'And the shovel couldn't dent it.' Katy was looking across the field, towards the school. Sophie turned to follow her gaze. The teachers were walking back, Mr McGowan carrying the box as if it were a baby. But Katy wasn't looking at them. She was looking at Ashton, who was standing in the shadow of the light-house. Brother and sister exchanged a meaningful glance before Ashton nodded once, turned and followed the teachers back into the school building.

Sophie's heart beat faster as she tried to understand what Katy was thinking.

'I think I know why they couldn't open the box,' said Katy.

'Why?' asked Sophie. What could Katy know about a box that had been underground for 300 years?

'I can sense something,' Katy whispered. 'There's magic inside that capsule.'

TWO

Sophie leaned on the edge of the sink in the Year 9 girls' bathrooms, watching her friends fussing around Kaz. Joanna held a sheet of instructions and Lauren was clutching her alarm clock.

Kaz peered into the mirror and adjusted the towel wrapped around her head. 'Are you sure you got the timing right? What if it dries out my hair and ruins it? That happened to my cousin.'

'Leave the dye in for thirty minutes, no longer. Then rinse your hair using the special conditioner,'

Joanna read. She glanced at her watch. 'Any minute now ...'

The alarm clock buzzed in Lauren's hand, making her squeak. 'Time's up!' Lauren told her.

Kaz rushed through the connecting door to the bath. As Kaz knelt beside the tub, Sophie lifted the shower-head and Erin turned on the water. Katy stood ready with another towel.

'Like your very own salon,' said Joanna with a giggle.

Kaz ducked her head under the water and washed the dye out. The water turned a dirty brown colour.

'Are you totally sure you got the time right?' Kaz asked as she reached for the towel.

'Positive!' Erin had a very serious look on her face. 'Kaz, there's no way we'd mess up something this important. It's your *hair*!'

Sophie and Katy exchanged a glance. Perhaps a little bit of magic wouldn't hurt ...

'Let me do that, Kaz.' Sophie took the towel from her and dried her friend's hair. As she did so, she murmured under her breath, 'Great forces of the Earth, give this hair the light of the summer sun!'

She closed her eyes and imagined she was on a beautiful beach, bathed in sunshine. As if it could read her thoughts, the Source on her finger tingled. A warm feeling spread up into her arms and all over her body, just as if she was being bathed by sunlight.

'What did you say, Sophie?' Erin looked puzzled.

Sophie's heart skipped. 'Oh, um, just humming to myself. You know, like a real hairdresser.' She took the towel away. Kaz turned to the mirror, looking miserable and nervous. The others looked hopefully at her hair. It didn't seem any different.

'Well, you sometimes can't tell until it's dry,' said Lauren.

Sophie smiled as a sudden shaft of sun came through the high window of the bathroom and lit up Kaz's hair. Beautiful golden glints sparkled all over it.

'. . . but I think it's going to look great!' Lauren finished with a grin.

Kaz ran off to the dorm to blow-dry her hair, with the others trailing after her anxiously. When Kaz straightened up and tossed back her hair, everyone gasped, even Sophie. Kaz's hair had gone the most beautiful colour – like sunbeams dancing on a summer day.

'Oh, Kaz, it looks gorgeous!' Joanna exclaimed. She glanced at the picture on the box. 'It's better than the model's!'

Kaz smiled at herself in the mirror. But then a worried expression came back over her face. 'What if—'

'Oh, *Kaz*!' everyone chorused in mock exasperation.

'What are you worried about now?' asked Sophie, laughing.

Kaz scrunched up her face. 'Guys, no, I'm really serious ... what if Oliver doesn't like it? What if he preferred me with *brown* hair?'

Sophie and Katy exchanged a glance. That was something they *couldn't* fix with magic.

When Sophie passed her mum's office on her way home she saw that the big Turlingham Hockey Cup was gone from the glass cabinet where it usually stood. In its place was the time capsule. A card notice stood in front of it. It read:

THIS TIME CAPSULE

WAS BURIED 300 YEARS AGO

BY BENEDICT WAPENTAKE,

THE FIRST MASTER OF TURLINGHAM.

WE ARE IN THE PROCESS

OF FINDING A WAY TO

OPEN IT WITHOUT CAUSING DAMAGE.

Sophie walked up to the glass and looked at the capsule. The box was not large, but it looked heavy. Gazing at it gave her a funny shiver down her back. Was Katy right? Was there really magic inside?

Gally, her squirrel familiar, poked his head out of her schoolbag. His nose twitching, he sniffed the air and looked at the capsule with bright eyes. The fur on his neck bristled and Sophie was sure she could feel him shivering.

'It's OK, Gally,' she whispered, patting him.

She frowned. She knew very well that magic could be used for good, but also for evil.

She took out her phone and texted Katy and

Callum quickly: I KNOW WHERE THE CAPSULE IS. LET'S FIND OUT IF KATY'S RIGHT!

Just as she pressed Send, she heard a squeal from inside her mum's office. Gally's ears pricked up and Sophie almost dropped her phone. Her mum sounded terrified.

She ran to the door and burst in. Her mum was flattened against the wall behind her desk while smoke poured out of the fireplace on the opposite side of the room.

'Mum! What happened? Are you OK?'

'It's doing it again!' her mum yelped, and pointed to the fire.

Sophie looked again. The smoke billowed into the room in a big gust, showering ashes everywhere, moving around as if it was alive. Sophie could see shapes forming inside it.

Her mum dodged around the desk and made for the fire alarm by the door, but Sophie grabbed her hand as she was about to press it. 'Wait, Mum!'

Sophie's mum looked at her as if she was crazy.

'I think . . . I think this might be magic.'

'*Magic!*' Her mum put a hand to her mouth. 'But ... in my office?'

Sophie felt guilty. Her mum had only known about magic for a few weeks. Sophie knew, from personal experience, that it was a weird one to get your head around.

'Sit down, Mum,' she said hurriedly, and pulled a chair over to her. Her mum collapsed into the chair, fanning herself with an Ofsted report. Sophie turned back to the fire. The smoke seemed to fight with itself, until a shape formed in the centre of it: an oblong, which became more and more solid. The rest of the smoke was sucked back up the chimney, and the oblong gently settled on the rug. Sophie watched as it slowly became something she recognised – an envelope.

She took the fire tongs and pulled the envelope towards her. It didn't seem to be hot, and it stayed solid, not like smoke at all. She reached out and picked it up. As she did so, the crescent-moon ring on her finger glowed orange in the reflected flames.

Sophie turned the envelope over. Letters that seemed to be made of fire danced on its surface.

For the attention of Mrs Morrow, Headmistress, Turlingham Academy, Norfolk.

'It's for you, Mum,' she said, turning round to hand it to her.

Her mum shrank back. 'Oh – er – could you open it, Sophie? You're more used to all this, this . . . *magic* . . . stuff than I am.'

Sophie opened the envelope, excited to see what it said. She'd never seen a magic letter like this before. A sheet of misty smoke rose out of it and hung in the air, quivering. There was writing on it.

Dear Mrs Morrow, Sophie read.

We are writing with regard to our daughter, Abbie. Abbie is currently in Year 9 at a local school, and doing well. However, we were excited to hear that Turlingham is sympathetic to witch students. I am sure you appreciate how difficult it is to find a school that is really supportive of difference – especially this particular one. We were therefore wondering if it would be possible to come and meet you and discuss sending Abbie

to Turlingham Academy? Please let us know at
your earliest convenience.
Sincerely,
Andrew and Amelia Clarke

Sophie squealed with excitement. Her mum jumped.

'Oh, Mum!' Sophie held out the sheet to her. 'Can she come? Please, can she?'

'Can who come? Come where?' Her mum took the sheet of smoke and read the letter.

Sophie hopped from foot to foot with impatience. She wanted another witch in the school so much! A girl her own age, who knew how it felt to be a witch! That would be amazing.

Of course Katy was the best friend ever, but witch hunter magic wasn't quite the same as witch magic, and even though Sophie's dad was a witch he was – well, her dad. There were so many things that only another witch her own age could understand, such as what it was really like having a Source, or how important a familiar was. Maybe they could even combine their magic!

'Andrew and Amelia Clarke . . .' her mum muttered. Then she gave a little yelp of surprise as the sheet of smoke wafted itself out of her fingers and back up the chimney.

'So, Mum? *Please?*'

'Well, Sophie, I . . . I . . . I just don't know.' She brushed off her hands, still eyeing the fire nervously. 'I'm not sure how I feel about Turlingham getting a reputation for taking in witches and witch hunters. There must be all kinds of complications.'

'But there aren't, really!' Sophie pleaded. 'I know it's hard to deal with at first, Mum. It was for me too, at first.'

'Yes,' her mum said. She reached out to give her a hug. 'I feel bad whenever I think of you having to make that discovery alone, Sophie. I know how much it would mean to you to have someone who could really understand here. But . . .'

Sophie hugged her back. 'Please, Mum,' she said. 'Just meet them. What harm can that do?'

Her mum ran her hands through her hair. 'OK then. We'll have the Clarkes round for dinner.' She shook her head. 'I would never have believed this when I was a young trainee teacher.'

Sophie smiled. She wouldn't have believed it a few months ago either – but she was really glad it had turned out that way.

THREE

Sophie burst out of the big school doors, letting them bang behind her. It was almost dark but she knew the way back to the cottage she shared with her mum and dad so well that she could have run there blindfold. She raced across the courtyard and through the trees, and pushed open the garden gate. She let herself in, shouting, 'Dad! Dad!' She couldn't wait to tell him the news. Another witch at Turlingham!

There was no answer from upstairs, so she opened the back door and made her way across the muddy back garden to the shed. A shadowy shape dropped from the fence and wound around her ankles with a mew.

'Mincing! You startled me.' She bent to rub the Siamese cat's head. 'Oh, are you moulting?'

Poor Mincing looked pretty scrawny, a shadow of his former sleek, arrogant self. Sophie felt sorry for him. He was her Aunt Angelica's familiar, and he hadn't been the same since she'd been demagicked. She gave him another stroke and then went up to the door of the shed and tapped on it.

'Come in,' said her dad.

Sophie pushed open the door. Her dad looked up from his work bench. His Source, a golden pocket watch, glinted on his jacket. There were candles burning all around the cosy room, and there were plants and bunches of dried herbs hung from the ceiling. It smelled of mint and lavender and cinnamon.

In a corner, tucked up in a wicker rocking chair, sat Sophie's Aunt Angelica, her unruly hair tamed into a long smooth plait. Sophie could see at a glance that there was no change in her condition: she gazed into the distance, as if she was in a trance. Mincing slipped past Sophie and leapt on to her lap with a pitiful mew. Aunt Angelica didn't stir. Sophie touched her hand gently, then turned to her dad.

'Oh, Dad, you won't believe it, this is so cool!' Sophie tumbled out her news about the letter from the witch family.

Her dad smiled. 'That's excellent! It'll be wonderful for you. If your mum agrees, that is,' he added.

'Please, Dad, can you send them a magic letter back? So it gets there really quickly?'

'Of course!' He turned back to the work bench and passed his fingers over the candle so that the flame wavered and lengthened. 'This is something you should learn to do, Sophie, so watch carefully.'

Sophie watched as he continued to weave his fingers in and out of the flame. His watch gleamed and reflected the flames as if it too was on fire.

'Earth, water, wind and fire,' her dad murmured. As he repeated the words, Sophie felt her skin tingle, and her hearing seemed to grow even stronger, so she could hear the earthworms in the ground turning over the soil, the shiver of blades of grass growing, fish swimming in the brook at the end of the garden. She held her breath. Magic was the best feeling ever. She glanced at her motionless Aunt Angelica, feeling deeply sorry for her. Demagicking was one of the worst things that could ever happen to a witch.

'Mighty forces of the Earth, give these words the power to seek and find their hearer,' her dad ended. He leaned close to the flame as if it were a microphone, and spoke into it. 'Dear Mr and Mrs Clarke. We would be delighted to meet you and discuss Abbie attending Turlingham Academy. Can you come for dinner on Monday? Yours sincerely, Franklin Poulter.'

He ended with a sharp puff of breath that Sophie thought would blow the flame out. But instead, it blew the flame *off* the candle. Sophie gasped as it floated across the shed like a soap bubble, leaving the dead wick behind it. Then the flame simply seemed to get further and further away as she watched – although she knew it was still inside the shed – until it became as tiny as a distant star and finally vanished altogether.

'There,' said her dad, breaking the silence. 'It'll reach them as quickly as an email would – and be a lot harder for witch hunters to trace!' He sighed and stretched. 'Let's go and get some tea ready for your mum.' He glanced wistfully at the candle as he stood up.

Sophie followed his gaze, then looked back at him as he went to gently help Angelica from her chair. She realised for the first time that his eyes were red, as if he had been crying.

'Dad? What's the matter?' She put a hand on his arm.

'I'm trying to find Rosdet.' He spoke lightly, but sadness lurked behind his words. 'I send a magic message, like a notice, out to witches, just in case someone has seen him.' He tucked Angelica's arm under his own and guided her to the door. She moved like a sleepwalker. Mincing trotted ahead of her, glancing up now and then as if to make sure she was safe. 'But no one has ever replied.'

Sophie's heart ached. Rosdet was her dad's familiar, a fine red fox. But they had been separated many years ago while he was on the run from the witch hunters. Sophie knew what it was like to be separated from someone you loved; it wasn't so long ago that her dad had been missing too. If only they could get Rosdet back, then their family would be properly complete.

'Do you still think there's a hope of finding him, then?' she said. Gally scrambled out of her bag, along her arm and on to her dad's shoulder. He nuzzled him gently, as if trying to comfort him, and Sophie's dad stroked him back, a sad look on his face.

'I can't give up on him.'

As they stepped out on to the path under the starry night sky, Sophie's dad hesitated.

'A bit of a breeze ... so there is one more thing I can try,' he said under his breath. He licked a finger and held it up in the air. 'West,' he said as if to himself. He turned so that he faced into the gentle wind that was blowing inland, and whistled. The whistle began low and gradually rose higher and higher until Sophie cringed and covered her ears, and then suddenly she could no longer hear it. From her dad's pursed lips, though, she could tell that he was still whistling. Then she thought she could hear the whistle echoing back from the stars and the brook and the leaves in the trees. It swept towards her on the wind, blew past her and disappeared. Gally sat on her shoulder, his ears pricked up, as if he could hear it long after she could.

'What was that?' Sophie whispered.

'A special magic call between me and Rosdet,' he said. He gazed in the direction that the wind was blowing. Sophie thought he looked very sad and lonely. 'The wind will carry the whistle and he'll know I'm looking for him.'

Sophie slipped her arm into her dad's, feeling deeply sorry for him. She couldn't imagine what would happen if she ever lost Gally.

'I bet he knows anyway, Dad,' she said as they walked back to the house. She was sure that Rosdet, wherever he was, knew how much her dad missed him. That is, if he was still alive.

No, I mustn't think like that, she thought to herself, *there's always hope. There must be.*

FOUR

'Mum, don't you think we ought to use the best glasses instead?' Sophie rushed into the kitchen from the dining room, Gally at her heels. She had just been setting the table, and she had spent ages folding the napkins. She wasn't sure why, but she really wanted to impress the Clarkes tonight.

Her mum, lifting a shepherd's pie from the oven, laughed through the steam.

'Oh goodness, Sophie, I don't think they'll mind!' She put the pie down and stuck a fork into the mashed potato. 'Mmm, smells good! Even if I say so myself.'

'It's going to be delicious, Mum.' Sophie headed over, hoping for a taste, but a ring at the doorbell made her change direction sharply. 'I'll get it!'

Sophie skipped into the hall. She recognised the two people through the frosted glass instantly: Katy and Ashton. She opened the door, beaming. 'Come in, come in!' She hugged Katy hello, and was so excited that she almost hugged Ashton too – but then realised what she was doing and pulled back with an embarrassed smile. 'Um ... they're not here yet. Any minute, though!'

As she closed the door she realised that both Katy and Ashton looked uncomfortable.

'Sophie, it was really nice of your mum to invite us round for dinner ...' Katy began, as she hung up her coat and scarf.

'... but why is she so keen for us to meet Mr and Mrs Clarke?' Ashton finished for her.

'I don't know.' Sophie laughed. 'But what does it matter? You get to eat my mum's famous shepherd's pie . . . Oh, hang on. It's not because they're witches, is it? You two aren't going to get all witch-huntery on me, are you?' Her face fell. 'I thought we were over that.'

Katy laughed, and even Ashton smiled. His voice was low and gravelly as he said, 'We don't have a problem with witches any more, Sophie. But that doesn't mean witches won't have a problem with us. If they picked this school because it was friendly to witches, I wonder how they'll feel about meeting two witch hunters at dinner with the headmistress.'

'Oh . . .' Sophie could see what he meant. But it was hard to feel too downcast. She was sure the Clarkes would love Katy – and maybe even Ashton too. Still, she was worried. She looked at Katy for reassurance, but Katy didn't smile.

Sophie held Katy back as Ashton went into the dining room.

'Katy? What's the matter?' she said in a low voice, looking into her face. 'Are you really worried about meeting them?'

Katy shook her head. 'No . . . it'll be fine. I'm sure. Like you said.'

'So what's up?'

Katy took a deep breath before saying, 'You've been talking about nothing but Abbie for the past week. You keep going on about how you're going to have so much in common and . . . well . . . three's a crowd, isn't it?'

'Katy!' Sophie was shocked; she hadn't realised Katy was worried about being left out. 'No way. You and me are like sisters. We've been through so much together. No one's ever going to come between us.' She took Katy by both shoulders. 'Ever.'

'Promise?' Katy half smiled.

'Promise.' Sophie held up her wrist to show she was wearing the friendship bracelet Katy had made for her. Katy smiled and tapped fists with her, so that her own friendship bracelet jingled. Sophie was about to remind Katy how much those bracelets stood for, but just then the doorbell rang again.

'That's them!' Sophie exclaimed, and ran to answer the door.

Sophie glanced around the dinner table. Mr and Mrs Clarke seemed nice, though Sophie was a little disappointed that Abbie hadn't come with them. At the head of the table, Angelica sat gazing into space, a lost, dreamy expression in her eyes. Sophie's dad was cutting up her food for her and feeding her. Mrs Clarke, a small woman with mousy hair, kept casting her sympathetic glances.

'So if Abbie came here she would benefit not only from our excellent pastoral care,' Sophie's mum continued to Mr Clarke, 'but a whole range of extra-curricular activities, such as our award-winning orchestra, sailing, involvement in the Earl of Turlingham Award—'

'Hmm, yes,' Mr Clarke said politely, blinking through his glasses. Unlike his wife, he was very tall, so tall he had to hunch to sit at the table. Sophie wondered which one Abbie would look like.

Ashton, who was sitting next to Mrs Clarke, leaned towards her with a charming smile. 'Would you care for some more shepherd's pie, Mrs Clarke?' He was clearly making an effort.

Mrs Clarke started. 'Oh ... er, thank you,' she squeaked.

Mr Clarke watched warily as Ashton spooned it on to her plate. He tried not to wince when Ashton's hand accidently brushed his as he was putting the dish down. Sophie caught Katy's eye across the table and knew they were thinking the same thing: the Clarkes weren't comfortable around witch hunters.

Mrs Clarke smiled thanks to Ashton, but her gaze went straight back to Angelica. Mincing was draped around her neck like a scarf. Mrs Clarke reached out and stroked him.

'It's a terrible shame,' she said, turning back to Sophie. 'Your poor aunt. I can't imagine who would do such a cruel thing. To demagick a witch, you would have to be . . . '

Sophie's dad cleared his throat and motioned towards Katy and Ashton. Mrs Clarke shut her mouth quickly.

Sophie swallowed. 'Actually,' she said, feeling her face go hot with embarrassment, 'it wasn't witch hunters who did this to her.' She felt a sickness rise in her. Guilt. 'It was me.'

Both Mr and Mrs Clarke put their knives and forks

down. Their eyes widened. Sophie swallowed the lump in her throat.

'And very bravely, too,' her dad said. 'I'm afraid Angelica was already quite deranged when it happened. If it wasn't for Sophie, my sister would have caused the deaths of many people.'

'Oh really?' Mr Clarke raised his eyebrows. 'I heard she was trying to kill witch hunters.'

'Witch hunters *are* people,' said Ashton, frowning.

Mr Clarke mumbled something and then went quiet.

Sophie's mum tried to fill the awkward silence by hastily describing the school. 'Of course our academic record is very strong. Our library is extremely well stocked—'

'Ah yes, the library!' Mr Clarke drew himself up. His eyes gleamed behind his small round spectacles and even his comb-over seemed to bristle with excitement. 'We have heard there is a magical library, beneath the ordinary one. Is this correct?'

'Well ... er ... yes, it is.'

Sophie thought her mum sounded a little thrown.

'It's famous throughout the witch community.' Mrs Clarke nodded enthusiastically. 'Would Abbie be able to have access to that library? Would we be able to see it?'

Sophie instinctively felt a little protective. She felt like it was *her* library.

'I don't see why not, right, darling?' Sophie's dad said enthusiastically before Sophie's mum had a chance to speak. He leaned over to talk to Mr Clarke. 'It's a superb collection of spell books and grimoires. Really one of the best in the world.'

'But you've got to be careful,' Sophie joined in. 'it's really easy to get lost. There's a spell on it that makes all the shelves move around. Me and Katy almost got stuck down there!'

Mr Clarke, who had just taken a sip of water, spluttered, 'Er . . . sorry, did you say that you, and er . . . ' He gestured to Katy. 'A *witch hunter*? In the magic library?'

Katy blushed, and Sophie frowned. 'Yes, why not?' she said coldly. Even if she did want Abbie to come to the school, she wasn't going to let the Clarkes be rude to her best friend.

'Oh, nothing, nothing.' Mr Clarke seemed lost for words.

Ashton, who was looking cross, opened his mouth, but to Sophie's relief her mum got there first.

'I'm glad this topic has come up,' she said. She had on what Sophie called her 'headmistress' expression. 'I invited Katy and Ashton here tonight for a reason. I want to make it clear that witch hunters, as well as witches, are welcome at this school.'

Katy smiled at her gratefully. Sophie couldn't love her mum any more than she did right now.

'Yes, but ...' Mr Clarke fingered the stem of his glass, a nervous expression on his face.

'Mrs Morrow,' said Mrs Clarke gently. 'As a human, I'm not sure you understand. The Gibsons have hunted the Clarkes for centuries. Such feelings are not easily—'

'It may not be *easy*,' said Sophie's mum, 'but it must be done. What happened in the past stays in the past. And unless you are able to accept that witch hunters attend this school, I am afraid Abbie will not be able to join us at Turlingham.'

There was silence. Sophie crossed her fingers under the table.

Mr and Mrs Clarke exchanged a thoughtful glance.

'Very well,' said Mrs Clarke. She smiled, and so did her husband. 'We promise to put aside our differences.'

Mr Clarke reached his hand out to Ashton. After a second, Ashton took it, and the two shook hands. Mrs Clarke and Katy also shook hands across the table.

Mrs Clarke looked back at Sophie's mum. 'We're very impressed with the school. In every way. We'll bring Abbie to you on Thursday – and I have every confidence that she will be extremely happy at Turlingham.'

Yay! Sophie felt like getting up and doing a dance. She tried to catch Katy's eye to share a smile, but Katy was looking the other way. But it'd be OK – Sophie just knew that when Abbie arrived they'd all get on like a house on fire.

FIVE

The common room was full of morning sun and morning chatter as everyone made the most of their last moments of freedom before classes started. Sophie was with her friends in their usual seats by the window, but she couldn't sit still. She got up to peer outside, searching the drive for any sign of the Clarkes' car pulling up.

'Sophie, what's the matter with you?' Erin asked, looking up from braiding Joanna's hair. 'You're jumping around like a newly formed boy band.'

'Abbie will be here any minute!' Sophie ran back to the group and slid into her chair. 'You remember what I said, right? We have to be really, really nice to her, OK?'

'Well, duh, it's not like we're usually horrible or anything.' Erin laughed and reached for another hairclip.

'Oh, I know, but pleeeeaaase make friends with her? For me?'

Lauren looked up from her beanbag. 'Of course we will,' she said, 'but why are you so worked up about it?'

'Oh, um ...' Sophie shrugged. Of course she couldn't tell them the real reason. 'I just have this feeling that we're going to have so much in common and she's going to fit into our gang perfectly and—'

Joanna laughed and Sophie looked up in time to see Katy roll her eyes.

She laughed too, feeling a bit embarrassed. 'OK,' she admitted, 'maybe I have been going on about Abbie a bit too much!'

'You've talked about nothing else ever since we heard she was coming,' Erin said. She nodded towards the corner of the room, where Kaz and Oliver were gazing into each other's eyes and talking in low voices. 'When we have other stuff to talk about . . . like how much Oliver loves Kaz's hair!'

'It turned out so well,' Katy said, and everyone agreed. As Sophie watched, Oliver stroked Kaz's newly blond hair *again*.

Erin put the finishing touches to Joanna's plaits and glanced over towards Mark, who was frowning in concentration into his mirror as he worked on getting his parting perfect. 'Maybe I should dye my hair too!'

The girls' laughter broke off as Mrs Freeman's stern voice rang out from the doorway. 'What's all this noise?'

Sophie looked up. Next to Mrs Freeman stood a tall, slim girl with the bluest eyes Sophie had ever seen. Her long, straight hair was a gorgeous rich, deep red – the colour of a glossy conker. She smiled shyly, showing pretty dimples and perfectly white teeth.

Oliver's mouth dropped open; he stopped stroking Kaz's hair and inched away from her a little. The dreamy smile faded from Kaz's face. Mark looked up from his mirror, and fumbled his comb. It fell to the floor with a clatter but he didn't seem to notice. He was too busy staring at the stranger.

'This is our new girl for Year 9, Abbie Clarke,' Mrs Freeman said. 'I'm sure you'll all make her very welcome. Would one of you please volunteer to show her around?'

A load of hands shot up. *Boys'* hands.

But Sophie went one better. She jumped out of her chair, and ran right up to Abbie. 'I'll do it, Mrs Freeman!' she announced.

Mrs Freeman took a step back. 'That's very kind of you, Sophie. Abbie, Sophie is Mrs Morrow's daughter. She knows the school better than anyone.'

Sophie gave Abbie a big hug. 'It's so cool to have you here!' she said. 'Finally!'

Then Sophie felt a bit silly. Had she just come on too strong? She didn't want to scare her off before she'd even had a chance to speak.

But Abbie hugged her back. 'And I'm so glad to be here!'

Sophie grinned at her.

The bell rang for the start of the first lesson, and everyone surged for the door. Sophie was swept up by her friends, and she and Abbie went along with them.

'So, do you two know each other from before or something?' Erin said, looking curiously at Abbie as they walked along the corridor.

Sophie exchanged a nervous glance with Abbie. Of course the others would be curious to know why they were *so* friendly. 'N-no,' she began, not wanting to lie. 'Umm ...'

But Abbie took over smoothly. 'Oh, your head-mistress is so nice. I just figured Sophie would be nice too, because she's her daughter.'

Sophie smiled in relief. Abbie could obviously think on her feet!

'Oh, right.' Erin didn't look convinced. 'But—'

'Abbie, I've got to show you your locker,' Sophie said hastily. 'It's just over here.' She linked arms with her and swerved towards the corridor where the lockers were.

'You'll be late for class, Sophie,' Katy called to her.

'We won't be long!' Sophie tossed over her shoulder. She pulled Abbie over to a quiet corner. She couldn't contain her excitement a second longer. 'I'm so glad you're here!' she said, jumping up and down. 'It's going to be so great having another witch in the school! Where's your familiar? Have you done lots of spells?'

'Hey, slow down!' Abbie giggled, her blue eyes sparkling. 'I'm so pleased to be here too. There weren't any witches in my last school either.'

'Sophie, why for are you dawdling?' Madame Leclerc came hurrying by, her nose just clearing a stack of exercise books, her French accent sounding even thicker than usual. 'You should be in my French lesson. *Vite, vite*, 'urry up!'

'Sorry, madame!' Sophie ran on to class and Abbie followed her, but hesitated at the door, looking shy.

She tugged at Sophie's sleeve. 'Can I sit next to you? It's just – I don't know anyone ...'

'Of course!' Then Sophie remembered Katy. Sophie always sat next to Katy for everything. 'I'm sure Katy won't mind.'

Sophie made her way over to Katy, hoping she would understand. 'Umm, Katy?'

Katy looked up at her, and when she saw Abbie standing next to her, her smile faded a little.

'Would you mind if I sat next to Abbie today?' she asked. 'It's her first day.'

Katy didn't look happy, but she said, 'I guess so,' and smiled at Abbie. Then she got up, gathered her books and moved to an empty desk in the next row.

'Aw, thanks, Katy!' Abbie called over.

Sophie felt a little bad, but she'd speak to Katy again later. She was sure Katy would understand when she got to know Abbie better.

'Settle down, girls.' Madame Leclerc came in behind them and put the books down. 'Today, we 'ave a film to watch. Can someone draw ze curtains please.'

Abbie and Sophie settled into their seats. As Madame looked for the remote control Abbie leaned towards Sophie. 'So . . . is Katy the witch hunter?' she whispered, looking over towards Katy's back.

Sophie leaned towards her and whispered back. 'Yes . . . and she's my best friend.'

Abbie nodded. Sophie's heart swelled to see she didn't seem to have a problem with witch hunters. *Abbie's going to fit in just fine*, she thought happily.

As the film went on, Sophie felt a piece of paper being pressed into her hand. Abbie was passing her a note. She opened it under the desk, and read: *Why don't we meet up tonight and hang out? Maybe we could try out some spells together . . . combine our powers?* ☺

Sophie's heart beat fast with excitement. This was exactly what she'd wanted to do! She'd only ever combined her spells with Katy, never cast spells with another witch. She quickly wrote back: *Yes! That would be great, can't wait to try out spells with you.*

She heard Katy clear her throat and looked up. Katy had seen the note, and tilted her head slightly. Sophie knew she wanted her to pass the note over, but Madame Leclerc had paused the film and was going over to open the curtains. It was too risky. She shook her head.

Katy raised her eyebrows and Sophie could see she was cross. She sighed and passed the note over to Katy just as Madame Leclerc turned to pull open the curtains.

Katy read it and Sophie saw a hurt expression cross

her face. Katy crumpled the note up and stuffed it into her desk. She didn't look back at Sophie.

Sophie couldn't help feeling a bit guilty, but she was annoyed too. After all, Abbie was the new girl – and Katy knew what that felt like. Katy had been the new girl not so long ago. Surely she should try a bit harder to be friendly. Especially when Sophie had said how much it meant to her.

'Now, class,' said Madame Leclerc, 'I would like you to write a review of the film, using your best French. You will finish it for homework and hand it in to my pigeonhole tomorrow morning please.'

As she wrote down the homework instructions Sophie suddenly realised why Katy was annoyed – she'd already made plans to investigate the time capsule with her and Callum that night. Hastily she scribbled another note to Abbie:

Sorry, I forgot – we're going to check out the time capsule later. Come along with me and Katy and Callum instead?

Abbie read the note, smiled and nodded.

Madame Leclerc handed out the exercise books.

Abbie opened up her pencil case and took out a glossy black pencil with a white lead. Sophie raised her eyebrows, and so did Madame Leclerc.

'Abbie, my dear, we usually use ballpoint pens here,' she said.

'Oh, please let me use it, madame.' Abbie flashed her a smile. 'It's my lucky pencil and my handwriting's not as good without it.'

Madame Leclerc smiled. 'Very well, for now. So long as it is legible.' She moved on.

Sophie began to write. French wasn't her best subject and she had to get up to use the class dictionary a lot. As she came back past Abbie's desk she noticed something odd – although Abbie was writing, nothing was coming out of her pencil.

Sophie opened her mouth to say something, but then, to her amazement, she saw words *were* appearing on Abbie's paper. They looked very familiar . . . They were the exact same words from her own page! She looked back and forth from her exercise book to Abbie's. As soon as she wrote a word, a few seconds later it appeared on Abbie's page.

Abbie was copying! And using magic to do it!

Sophie didn't want to upset Abbie on her first day – but cheating was totally not OK! She sat down, whispering, 'Abbie, stop it!'

Abbie looked up. She didn't seem guilty at all. 'But I'm really bad at French,' she whispered back.

'Well, I'm not much good either,' Sophie whispered back, feeling annoyed. She was doing all the hard work and Abbie was taking all the credit. 'Madame Leclerc will know you've copied.'

'*Please*, Sophie.' Abbie made big eyes at her. 'Just till I catch up?'

Sophie sighed. 'OK – just this time,' she whispered.

'Thanks, Sophie!' Abbie smiled at her sweetly and went on pretending to write.

Sophie continued with the work, realising as she did so that she would have to do it all over again that evening so that it didn't look the same as Abbie's. She sighed. If only Abbie had known how much trouble she was causing her, she wouldn't have copied. She wouldn't be *that* mean, surely.

SIX

Sophie tiptoed down the dark Science corridor, making almost no noise in her trainers. A floorboard creaked and she jumped. If she was caught walking around the school at midnight, she'd be in big trouble! She stopped and listened, but she heard nothing else.

'Nothing to worry about, Gally,' she whispered to her squirrel, who was perched on her shoulder. She could feel his tail quivering against her cheek – Gally loved adventures!

She pushed open the door to the Biology lab and

went in. The plastic skeleton hanging in the window grinned at her. She patted him on the skull.

'Guys?' she whispered. 'Are you in here?'

The door to the store cupboard opened a crack and Callum peered out. He saw her and came out of the cupboard, Katy following him. Sophie smiled at her but Katy's answering smile took a few seconds to come. She folded her arms and hung back as Callum came eagerly up to Sophie.

'This is so cool! My first witch adventure. You really think there's magic in the capsule? Witch magic?' Callum was bubbling with excitement and it only made Katy's silence stand out the more. Sophie managed to catch her eye and Katy finally spoke.

'I'm surprised you're here, Sophie. I thought you had plans to meet up with Abbie.'

'Well, I thought . . .' She tailed off as the lab door opened behind her. Abbie walked in. Her hair was looped up in a messy bun – Sophie noticed she was using her special pencil as a hairpin. Katy looked startled, then blushed.

'Hey, guys,' said Abbie, dimpling. 'So, this is exciting!'

Sophie noticed a little blue butterfly dancing around her, and at the same moment Callum exclaimed, 'A butterfly! Wonder how that got in.'

'Oh, this is Mia,' Abbie said. She stretched out a slim finger, and the butterfly fluttered down and settled on it. It was the exact colour of Abbie's eyes.

'Your familiar!' Sophie exclaimed. 'Wow, she's beautiful!'

Gally ran across the desks and sat up to sniff gently at Mia. The butterfly moved her antennae, as if she were waving hello to him.

'Look,' said Sophie, 'they're making friends. How sweet!'

Callum took a step towards the animals. 'Do all witch's familiars do that?'

Katy interrupted them with a deep sigh. 'We'd better hurry up. Before anyone notices we're not in bed.'

Callum turned as if he had forgotten Katy was there. He took a step back and put his arm around her. 'The capsule is in the display case where the Hockey Cup used to be,' he said, 'by the head teachers' offices.'

Katy started following Callum and Abbie out of the lab, but Sophie caught her arm and drew her back. Katy turned and frowned at Sophie.

Sophie held out her arm. The friendship bracelet glinted on her wrist as she placed it next to Katy's matching one.

'Remember these?' she said.

'Of course.' Katy looked puzzled. 'You made one for me, and I made one for you.'

'That's right. And you put a magnet in mine so I'd be defended against witch hunter spells, and I put my favourite gold daisy earring in yours so you'd be defended against witches.' Sophie squeezed Katy's hand in her own. 'So you and me, Katy, we're not just friends – we're best friends for ever. No one, witch or witch hunter, is ever going to come between us. So don't worry!'

Katy blushed, and then smiled and flung her arms around Sophie in a hug.

'You're right, Sophie,' Katy said. 'I'm sorry for sulking. I'm not really jealous of Abbie ... I was just being silly.'

'Forget about it!' Sophie hugged her back, glad everything was sorted out. 'Come on, let's go. We can't let Callum and Abbie get there first!'

Callum and Abbie didn't seem to have missed them, and as the two girls caught up with them Callum laughed out loud at something Abbie had said. Abbie turned back to Sophie, Mia fluttering and dancing around her.

'So tell me about this time capsule. I wasn't here when it was dug up. What makes you think there's magic in it?'

Sophie looked at Katy and nodded at her to answer.

Katy cleared her throat, sounding embarrassed. 'Well, I – um – because I'm a witch hunter, I sort of sense when magic's around,' she said. 'I sensed it in the capsule.' Sophie already knew Abbie was fine with her being a witch hunter, but she could tell Katy was nervous about how Abbie would react.

'Wow,' Abbie breathed, her large eyes shining. 'You actually *sense* magic?'

'Um . . . well, yes,' Katy mumbled.

'Cool . . .' Abbie nodded thoughtfully as they turned the corner from the Science corridor and went through the big doors into the hall. The portraits of old head-mistresses and headmasters stared down at them as they crossed the stone-flagged floor. 'I get it. It's like our special hearing, you know,' Abbie said. 'The way me and Sophie can hear things from a long way away. I love how similar witches and witch hunters are.'

Sophie beamed.

'So, you want to do tests on the capsule to find out what sort of magic is inside?' Abbie went on. 'That's what I'd do.'

'Yeah, we have some tests planned.' Katy nodded to the big rucksack Callum was carrying. 'The most important thing to find out is whether it's good or bad magic inside.'

'You think it might be bad magic?' Abbie looked startled. 'And you're still going to investigate it? Aren't you scared?'

Callum shrugged. 'Well, we've got to make sure no one gets hurt, right?'

'Wow. You're *really* brave!' Abbie looked right at Callum as she spoke, and Callum blushed.

They hurried down the corridor towards the head teachers' offices. Sophie was nervous, but she knew they had to get to the capsule before the teachers opened it. If it was full of bad magic ...

She gasped as she saw the glint of glass on the floor around the display case.

'Look!' She pointed and broke into a run. The others followed her. They came to a shocked halt at the display case. The glass was shattered and scattered. Inside the cabinet there was ... nothing.

Someone had got there before them. And stolen the time capsule.

SEVEN

Sophie jolted awake. It was still dark, but someone was shaking her gently, whispering her name. She yawned and rubbed her eyes.

'Sophie! Wake up!' Her dad's voice seethed with excitement.

Sophie sat up, blinking. 'Dad? What's the matter?'

For a second she wondered if he'd found out about the stolen time capsule. She hadn't told her parents when she'd crept in just a few hours ago: if she'd told them about the time capsule, she would have to admit about the sneaking out too.

'Is everything OK?' she asked, testing the water.

In the moonlight she saw that her dad was wearing black jeans and a black sweater. He let her go, hurried to her wardrobe and pulled out a hoodie and jeans. He tossed them to her. Sophie, still half asleep, caught them.

'Get dressed, quick!' he hissed at her. 'I got a response from my message about Rosdet. I know where he is!'

Sophie jumped out of bed and tugged her clothes on as fast as she could. Gally sprang up on to her shoulder as if he could read her mind.

We have to save Dad's familiar!

The car drew to a halt at the verge of a wood. Sophie heard an owl hooting in the distance. They had been driving for what seemed like hours, but it was still dark.

'Where are we?' she whispered.

'I'm not sure. All this land belongs to a powerful witch hunter.' He undid his seatbelt and opened the door. 'The message was from a witch who was passing through a few days ago. He said we'd find Rosdet here.'

Sophie got out too. It was cold, and she could feel frozen tyre ruts in the mud underfoot.

Her dad flashed his torch into the undergrowth.

'Dad, look. I think there's a track there,' Sophie whispered.

Her dad gave her a thumbs-up and gestured for her to follow him through the undergrowth. Brambles tugged on her trousers and scratched her hands, but after a few metres they came to a high chickenwire fence. It was topped with barbed wire, and a security camera perched on one of the posts winked a red eye. Beyond it was an ugly concrete building with no windows. Sophie shivered; it didn't look like a friendly place. She hoped Rosdet was OK.

Sophie's dad switched off his torch and Sophie did the same.

'We'll have to bring this fence down somehow,' her dad whispered. He scanned the ground, and then bent to pick a leaf of ivy.

'Powers of the Earth. Earth, water, wind and fire.

Use your great strength to bring down this fence!' he whispered, twirling the leaf in his fingers.

There was a brief pause, as if the world was gathering its breath, and then a rustling noise began all around them. Sophie glanced up and around, wondering what was happening, then stifled a shriek as something slithered past her ankles. The ivy tendrils were growing, snaking across the ground towards the fence. As she watched, the tendrils hooked on to it and clambered up the wire. Thicker and greener and faster the ivy grew, until with a groan the wire gave way. The fence toppled forwards, ripping itself out of the concrete posts. The security camera crashed down in a bed of ivy and was quickly covered up.

They were in!

Sophie realised she had been holding her breath and let it out in a sigh of awe. Her dad, his eyes gleaming, picked his way across the fallen fence. Sophie followed him. *Rosdet, we're coming to get you!* she thought to herself. It had all been pretty easy.

Then a siren went off. Dogs started barking.

Oh no! Sophie's heart started beating fast in terror. Her dad caught her arm and ran with her into the shadows by the wall of the building. A few seconds later a man who looked like a security guard ran past. The man gasped when he saw the fallen fence, and stopped still. Sophie could feel Gally trembling in her pocket. This was a lot more dangerous than sneaking around the school at midnight!

Sophie's dad pointed to a metal ladder that ran up the side of the building. As the guard stared at the fence, they edged towards the ladder. The barking began again and suddenly another guard came around the corner of the building, with two slavering Rottweilers on short leashes.

Sophie gasped. The dogs would sniff them out! Sophie's dad began to mutter a spell under his breath, but Gally was quicker. Sophie felt him push out from her pocket and leap on to the ground.

'Gally, no!' Sophie hissed. She was about to run after him but her dad held her back. Gally raced across the compound, right under the noses of the dogs.

With a bark and a howl of excitement, the dogs tore

after Gally – who led them out through the broken fence and into the woodland.

'Hey!' shouted the guard, almost pulled off his feet as he ran to keep up with them.

Gally was so brave! She couldn't believe her little familiar had done that for her. Knowing it was their only chance to escape, she ran to the ladder, but as she climbed she kept glancing back over her shoulder to try and see Gally. If the dogs caught up with him … she didn't dare to think what would happen.

As they reached the roof she saw that there was a skylight in it.

They crouched as they ran across the roof. Her dad stamped on the skylight and the glass shattered. Luckily, the sound was covered by the wailing alarms.

'In here – quick!' He wrapped his jacket round his arm and pushed the broken glass out of the way, then slid himself through. Sophie saw him drop to the floor and he reached up to help her down. Her stomach lurched with fear and excitement as her dad caught her and lowered her to the ground.

Sophie's dad flashed his torch over the room. All

around her, wire walls rose to the ceiling. Cages. Inside them were animals – Sophie saw a deer, an eagle, several dogs and a hairless Sphynx cat, even some spiders in a tank. Sophie gasped and put a hand to her mouth. The place smelled of cooped-up animals, fear, and filthy bedding. But the animals weren't panicking at the intrusion. Instead they were watching Sophie and her dad intently.

Sophie felt disgusted. She understood what this place was, what these animals were, even before her dad said anything.

He drew in his breath and sounded shaken as he said, 'So the message was right – it's a testing lab. For familiars.'

Sophie was on the brink of tears. 'We've got to get them out, Dad!'

'I came for Rosdet.' He pursed his lips and blew the whistle that she had heard before.

'But Dad—'

'The guards will be back any minute, Sophie!' He raced off into the maze of cages, calling Rosdet's name. Sophie bit back tears. A fawn gazed at her with big, mournful eyes. Its cage was so small that it couldn't even stand straight. There was no way she could leave it there.

Sophie tried the door of the fawn's cage, but it was locked. She looked around but there was nothing to do magic with, no plants, nothing natural here at all. That was part of the reason why this place felt so horrible, she realised.

She jumped as a weight landed on her shoulder, and something cold and jangly was thrust against her ear.

'Gally!' she yelped. She didn't mean to make a noise, but she was so glad to see he was safe. She reached up and took the bunch of keys. 'You're amazing!'

She unlocked the fawn's cage and opened the door. It darted out, then wobbled a little before making its way to the other cages and sniffing at the animals. Sophie ran around the room, opening all the cages. The animals scrambled and trotted and jumped and wriggled out as soon as the doors swung open. All were still perfectly silent, as if they knew their lives depended on it. The dogs surged to Sophie to butt her hand gratefully with their wet noses, the cats wound themselves around her ankles and even the spiders seemed to want to thank her.

Over all the confusion, Sophie could still hear her dad calling for Rosdet.

'He has to be here somewhere!' he said as she caught up with him. There were tears in his eyes.

Sophie heard the snarling of dogs, getting closer. 'Dad, we have to go—' She broke off and whirled round as she heard a noise above them.

A guard stuck his head down through the broken skylight. 'Hey! What's going on? The beasts are loose!' he shouted to someone outside.

Sophie's dad gave one last, desperate whistle. And Sophie heard a distant, frantic baying.

Rosdet? she wondered.

Her dad raced towards the noise, sending empty cages flying as he flung them aside. Sophie ran after him. There, in a cage by the big steel doors, was a fox. He was big, with a black-tipped ear, and the tip was missing from his tail. Just how her dad had always described him.

The fox was pacing back and forth in his tiny cage, and his fur was rubbed thin in patches from pushing against the bars.

'Rosdet!' her dad shouted.

Sophie hurried to unlock the cage. The fox looked at her directly in the eyes, and as soon as he was released he leapt out into Sophie's dad's arms. Sophie's dad was laughing and crying at the same time. 'It's him! Rosdet! My boy ...'

Sophie felt a lump in her throat, so big it was hard to breathe. She thought she had never seen her dad so happy since he'd been able to come out of hiding and been reunited with Sophie and her mum. But she didn't have the time to celebrate. The big doors were opening.

'Dad, there's a guard at the skylight *and* one at the door. We're trapped!'

But as soon as the doors opened, all the animals charged for the exit. Sophie caught a glimpse of the guard's horrified face before the familiars burst out of the doors. He threw himself out of the way, tripped and fell to the floor, his arms up over his face to protect himself from being trampled. Sophie's dad grabbed her wrist and, with Gally and Rosdet racing alongside, they hurtled past the guard and out of the building with the familiars.

The thundering of hooves, pattering of paws and fluttering of wings was all around them as they sprinted through the broken fence. As soon as they reached the car, Sophie's dad pulled the door open and Sophie, Rosdet and Gally leapt into the back seat. Sophie's dad jumped into the driver's seat and revved the engine. Sophie, glancing back through the rear windscreen as they drove away, glimpsed the security guards, gasping for breath, break out of the trees and stand watching them drive away, while all around them the animals burst through the bracken, swung through the trees and flew through the sky. Back to the witches who loved them.

EIGHT

By the time they pulled into their driveway the sky was beginning to lighten. Sophie's fear had melted away. She felt as if she was fizzing inside with excitement, like a bottle of cola.

'I can't believe we did that, Dad!' she squeaked as the car came to a halt. 'Gally was so brave!'

'He was a hero – right, Rosdet?' Her dad turned off the engine and leaned lovingly over to stroke Rosdet once again. The fox looked exhausted but lowered his ears to be patted. 'Did you see the parrots? When they all flew up through the trees!' He turned to look at Sophie. 'You were right to set them all free. I'm proud of you.'

Sophie got out, Gally perching on her shoulder. Her dad reached out to pick Rosdet up, but he jumped down and padded after them.

'Phew! I must be getting old, though!' her dad went on, opening the front door. 'It's a long time since I've had an adventure like that.'

Sophie blinked in the unexpected glare from the hall light, and then she saw why it was on. Her mum was standing in the hall in her dressing gown, arms folded and a frown on her face.

'Oh ... Tamsin! You're up,' her dad said. He stopped at the door.

'Yes, I am,' her mum said. She spoke quietly but there was an edge to her voice. 'And so are you. And so – more importantly – is Sophie. At four a.m. on a school night!'

Uh-oh, Sophie thought. Suddenly she realised she was exhausted. She put her hand up to cover a huge yawn.

'Oh. I ... er ... ' Her dad shuffled his feet.

'You don't think, do you? You never do! You—'

'Mum, calm down.' Sophie pleaded. 'It was for a really good reason.'

Her mum's hands went to her hips. 'What could possibly be—'

'Look!' said Sophie.

Sophie's dad stood aside and Rosdet walked gingerly into the house. He glanced around him sharply, his ears flicking back and forth. Mincing, who had been watching from under the sideboard, hissed and spat and ran into the kitchen.

Sophie's mum gasped.

'I knew you'd be amazed,' Sophie's dad said proudly, closing the door behind them. 'It's Rosdet. I've found him, after all this time—'

'It's a fox,' Sophie's mum said, in a strangled voice. 'Franklin, foxes have fleas!'

Sophie's dad laughed, but stopped when he saw that Sophie's mum wasn't joining in. 'Oh, no, not this one,' he said eagerly. 'He's a familiar. *My* familiar.'

'Yes, Mum, it's not the same as a wild animal,' Sophie joined in.

'Sophie, foxes are not pets!' Sophie's mum clutched her head. 'We can't possibly keep one in the house. Are you telling me this night-time escapade was on behalf of a fox?'

'He's not any ordinary fox!' Sophie protested. Sophie's mum knew all about Rosdet from her dad, he spoke about him a lot. But Sophie realised she would never understand the importance of a familiar. How could she? 'Rosdet is a—'

'Yes, yes, you said.' Sophie's mum shook her head wearily. 'I'm afraid this is all too much for me.'

'Oh, darling.' Sophie's dad moved to hug her, but she stepped back.

'I know it's difficult, Mum,' Sophie began, remembering how hard it had been for her when she first found out Sophie was a witch. 'But if you could just try—'

'No, Sophie. It's you who must understand.' She bent down and put both hands on her shoulders. 'Your dad has taken you out, in the middle of the night, without a thought for school tomorrow, let alone your safety.' Sophie's mum spoke calmly but firmly. 'You must both promise me that there is to be no more magic.'

Sophie gasped.

'Not in the house, nor in the school. Not at all!'

'Mum, you can't ask that!'

'It's not a request,' her mum said sternly.

'But—' Sophie's dad began.

Sophie's mum turned to him, frowning. 'No, Franklin! Animals everywhere, warring witches and witch hunters – your own sister has had her life destroyed. She's catatonic!' She took a deep breath and calmed her voice. 'I understand that being a witch is something to do with who you are, but I will not have my daughter's life endangered.' She fixed Sophie with a steely gaze. 'No more magic. Promise.'

Sophie looked back and forth from her mum to her dad. There was no way of pleasing them both.

'I . . . promise,' she said miserably.

'Thank you,' her mum said. 'Now go to bed and try to get some sleep.'

Sophie trudged up the stairs. She could hardly believe what she had just said. No magic! It was like asking her to switch off the sun, turn off the sea. But the worst thing of all was that as she shut the door she could still hear her parents' angry, raised voices downstairs.

Sophie cracked another wide yawn as she walked down the corridor. Last night had been thrilling, but this morning she was so tired she could hardly keep her eyes open. *Maybe Mum had a point*, she thought wearily.

Sophie trooped on to the stage with the others and got in line between Joanna and Lauren.

'I can't believe there was a burglar sneaking around the school while we were all asleep,' Joanna said. 'That's creepy!'

It took Sophie a moment to realise what she was talking about. It felt like a week ago that the time capsule had disappeared, but of course it had only been last night.

'It might have treasure in it!' said Lauren. 'They'll have sold it. It'll be miles away by now.'

Sophie's head buzzed with thoughts. Had someone

really sold it to make money? She hoped it was that simple.

'Sophie!' Katy waved to her from where she was standing with the others. Sophie smiled and waved back. Katy looked upset, and Sophie thought it might be because of the capsule ... but as she reached them she realised it might have more to do with the fact that Abbie had all the boys grouped around her.

Abbie tossed her long red hair and Sophie picked up the end of what she was saying. '*I* wouldn't want to be in a relationship.' She batted her eyelashes at Mark, who blushed and grinned. 'Yeah, it's much more fun to be free and single!'

Erin, who was standing behind Abbie, caught Sophie's eye and scowled furiously, rolling her eyes towards Abbie.

Kaz crossed her arms, looking annoyed. 'Actually,' Kaz said, 'being in a relationship is great. I really enjoy it.'

'Um,' Sophie started, trying to think of a way to rescue the situation. 'I think what Abbie's trying to say is that there are really good things about being in a relationship *and* about being single.'

Abbie nodded, but Sophie could tell she wasn't really listening. She was trying to catch Oliver's eye – and she managed. She gave Oliver a dazzling smile. Then she glanced at her phone and laughed.

'Hey, my cousin just texted me this really funny joke. What do UFOs and intelligent blondes have in common?' The girls stared at Abbie. What was she going to say next? 'They don't exist.'

Kaz gasped.

'Hey, Abbie,' said Sophie, shocked. 'Kaz has just dyed her hair blond.'

'Yeah, what are you trying to say?' Erin put an arm around Kaz.

'I didn't mean *you*, Kaz!' Abbie laughed.

'Settle down please, everyone!' shouted Mrs Richardson. 'Now, you remember what we were practising last week? Let's begin with a rousing chorus.'

Sophie hoped that would be the end of it. She'd have to explain to Abbie that at Turlingham it was friends first, boys second. She dropped her shoulders, relaxed, lifted her head up and began to sing with the others. Although she was focusing, it was hard to miss the fact that someone nearby was completely out of tune. She glanced along the row. *Abbie!*

As the song came to an end Kaz whispered to Sophie: 'Great hair – pity about the voice!'

Sophie caught Abbie's eye as she spoke. *Uh-oh.* She could tell from the change in Abbie's expression that she had overheard. She nudged Kaz, who blushed.

'Sorry, Abbie. I . . . I . . .'

To Sophie's relief Abbie just laughed as they sat down and said: 'I know, it's bad, isn't it? Everyone says I've got a voice like a strangled duck.'

Sophie giggled, and Kaz smiled grudgingly.

Mrs Richardson flipped through the pages of the song book while the choir shuffled and whispered. She looked up. 'As you know, we're trying to represent both the male and female voices equally, so for "The Power of Love" it makes sense to have a male and female duet. This will be the highlight of the concert – our grand finale.' She looked around at the choir, smiling. 'I think we'll have the auditions in our next rehearsal.'

Excited whispers broke out like forest fires all around. Abbie leaned across Erin to Sophie.

'Sophie, your voice is lovely. You ought to audition for the girl's part!' she said.

'Yes, Sophie, go for it,' Katy echoed her.

'Oh, I don't know.' Sophie felt shy. 'There'll be older girls auditioning too. I'll never get it.'

'Of course you will!' Abbie said enthusiastically. 'And I wonder who'll get the boy's part?' She glanced over to where Oliver was sitting. 'Do you think Oliver would go for it?'

'Well, if Oliver *did* get the boy's part,' said Sophie, thinking she'd better try and lay down some subtle ground rules for Abbie, 'we'd all try really hard to make sure Kaz got the girl's part. Right, girls?'

'Yeah,' said Erin, with a sharp look at Abbie. The others joined in.

Sophie looked at Abbie to see if she'd got the point, but Abbie's eyes were fixed on the door. Ashton had just walked in. Sophie had a sudden, sinking feeling in her stomach. She glanced back at Abbie, who was still staring at Ashton as he went over to Mrs Richardson, apologising for being late. She nodded and he strolled over to join the Year 10 boys on the chairs below. He glanced up to where the girls were sitting, his dark-lashed green eyes glinting like leaves in a shadowy forest.

'Who's *that*?' she murmured.

Sophie swallowed. She knew it wasn't any of her business . . . she knew she *definitely* didn't care about Ashton . . . but she was suddenly so, so sure that she didn't want Ashton to go out with Abbie.

'He's gorgeous!' Abbie said under her breath. She took Sophie's arm and drew her closer. 'Sophie, you know everyone in the school, why don't you introduce me?'

'G-gorgeous? Him?' Sophie laughed nervously. 'Really?'

'Of course! I mean, I bet all the girls in the school fancy him, don't they?' Abbie twirled a strand of her hair, eyes still fixed on Ashton. 'But I don't mind a challenge.'

Sophie felt dread in the pit of her stomach. She had to stop this. 'I don't know. I don't think he's all that, really.' Ashton was lounging on the chairs below her, and Sophie wished he hadn't chosen that moment to laugh at something Oliver said and make himself look even more handsome than normal.

Abbie glanced at her, a disbelieving look on her face.

'Come on, Sophie, are we looking at the same boy? He's lush! Look at that black hair and those green eyes and—'

'Yeah, but . . . ' Sophie squirmed. 'I just think he's a bit obvious, you know? A bit *too* good-looking. Too perfect.'

'Too *perfect*.' Abbie arched an eyebrow as Ashton laughed again, and pushed his sleek black hair out of his eyes. 'Interesting point of view! I guess being *too perfect* is definitely a flaw, but I'll try and forgive him for it.' She giggled and nudged Sophie.

Sophie laughed unhappily. Then she had an idea. One way to stop Abbie going for Ashton. 'You know he's Katy Gibson's brother, right?' she said.

'Oh!'

'Yeah, and you know what that means.' Sophie leaned in and whispered, 'Witch hunter.'

Abbie pulled a face like she wanted to be sick, then blinked it away and shrugged. 'Oh well, too bad. I don't care about Katy, of course, but there's a limit, isn't there? There's no way a witch could go out with a witch hunter. No. Way.'

Why did that statement make Sophie feel saddest of all?

They began to sing again, and this time Sophie realised that someone in the boys' group had a really good voice. She glanced along the row. To her surprise, it was Callum. She'd never really heard him sing before, but he was really, really good.

She turned to see if Katy had noticed – and saw Abbie. She was looking straight at Callum as if there was no one else in the room. There was a gleam in her eye.

Sophie gulped. She could sense danger. And this time it had nothing to do with magic.

NINE

Sophie didn't know how she managed to stay awake through the rest of the lessons, but she did. Just about. After the bell had rung, she waited for Katy by the old oak tree, the cold air keeping her from falling asleep on her feet. They had to discuss what to do about the missing capsule. People ran and shouted in the court-yard, or stood around talking. Distantly, through the crisp air, Sophie could hear a game of football on the playing field.

Sophie closed her eyes, thinking she would just rest

her head against the tree for a moment. Almost at once footsteps crunched close to her, and she opened her eyes to see Katy. Her cheeks were pink and her eyes were bright as if they were full of tears. Sophie was suddenly wide awake.

'What's the matter?' She put a hand on Katy's arm.

Katy shook her head, her mouth turning down. 'My parents didn't call today. Or yesterday. It's been ages.'

Sophie's head started to spin. Katy's parents had been ostracised from the witch hunter community for helping Sophie and her dad. What if something had happened to them? 'Can't you call them?'

'They didn't leave any contact details. They said it was safer if we didn't know where they were.' She rubbed a gloved hand across her eyes. 'They promised they'd call every other day, and it's been almost a week. I just keep imagining—' She broke off into a sob.

'Oh Katy, no! I'm sure they're safe.' Sophie *wasn't* so sure, but she knew that what Katy needed was comfort. She put an arm around her and they walked, their heads close together, towards the woods.

Katy was pulling nervously at a thread of her gloves. 'What if the witch hunters have got them and are punishing them somehow? What if they've killed—'

Sophie took both of Katy's hands and turned her firmly round to face her. 'You mustn't think like that. We've got to be positive.' Sophie motioned to Katy's gloves. 'And there's no point in unravelling your gloves, that won't help.' She gently took Katy's hand away from the thread.

Katy half laughed, half sobbed. 'I just hate not knowing.'

Sophie remembered what it had been like when her own dad was missing. 'I know,' she said softly. She hugged Katy tightly and Katy hugged her back.

Over Katy's shoulder Sophie saw a boy running down the path towards them. It was Ashton. Her heart jumped when his green eyes met hers. She let Katy go and they turned to him.

'Katy!' Ashton shouted. 'It's fine! They called – just now – Mum and Dad—'

Sophie's hopes lifted as Ashton came to a panting halt beside her.

Katy could hardly speak. 'What's happened? Where are they? Are they OK?' she asked.

'Relax.' Ashton grinned. 'They're safe, both of them.'

Katy stayed silent for a moment, then burst into tears.

'Hey, hey, Katy. Calm down,' Ashton said. He came in to hug Katy tight. Sophie stood back. She couldn't stop smiling; not just because Mr and Mrs Gibson were safe, but because Ashton was being so nice to his sister.

'I'm just relieved,' Katy sobbed on to Ashton's shoulder. 'I was so worried.'

'It's OK, Katy.' Ashton stroked her hair. 'It's going to be fine, I promise. Mum and Dad are really smart. The smartest people I know. They won't let anything bad happen to them.'

Katy stepped back, rubbed her nose, and searched for a tissue. 'You're absolutely sure it was them you spoke to?' she asked anxiously.

'Of course.' Ashton looked puzzled. 'Who else could it have been?'

Katy shrugged and looked at Sophie. 'I don't know. Maybe they've been taken and the person who has taken them is using some kind of possession spell.' She gave a weak smile. 'I know I'm being ridiculous. I can't help it.'

Ashton and Sophie laughed, then smiled at each other.

Sophie rubbed her friend's back. 'I think you might be worrying too much. Letting your imagination run away with you.'

Ashton nodded. 'Sophie's right. And anyway, possession is witch magic. No witch hunter would ever use it.'

Katy finally let herself laugh. 'Well, that's a relief. Thanks for coming to tell me, bruv,' she said with a sniff.

Ashton squeezed her shoulder. 'That's what big brothers are for,' he said with an awkward smile. He glanced shyly at Sophie and added, 'Come on, I'll buy you both a hot chocolate at the tuck shop. We need to celebrate.'

'Thanks,' Sophie said. As they walked back along the path towards the school she hoped he knew that it wasn't just the hot chocolate she was thanking him for: she was thanking him for being so nice to Katy. This was a side of him she hadn't seen before. And one she was beginning to like.

Sophie woke suddenly. After being so tired she was in a really deep sleep. But she could hear voices downstairs in the hall. One was her mum, but the others she couldn't quite recognise.

'We're so terribly sorry to disturb you at this time of night.'

Sophie sat up, suddenly wide awake. Abbie's parents? What were they here for?

'Do come in.' Her mum sounded flustered. 'What's the emergency?'

'Yes, do come in,' Sophie's dad urged. Sophie heard muffled conversation and then the front door shut. The Clarkes came through the hall towards the sitting room.

Sophie heard Mr Clarke say, 'We'd like to ask you something very important.'

Sophie looked at Gally, who was sitting on the end of her bed, just as upright and curious. She nodded to the door, and Gally jumped down. They tiptoed out of the room and down the stairs. Sophie's mum was just turning to close the sitting-room door. Sophie glimpsed the back of Mr Clarke's head behind her.

'No, of course you're not disturbing us,' Sophie's mum was saying. Then she spotted Sophie. Sophie smiled hopefully, but her mum raised her eyebrows, whispered, 'Bed!' and shut the door. Sophie sighed and Gally's tail drooped.

But she hesitated on the stairs. She knew she could overhear what was being said inside if she tried hard. She listened, and her strong witch hearing picked up voices at once. And that wasn't really magic, was it? It wasn't like casting a spell.

Mrs Clarke was speaking. 'We wanted to ask you a favour. Would you allow us to organise an anniversary party of our own? You see, the magical library is extremely important to the witch community.'

'The magical ... ' Sophie's mum didn't sound pleased, and Sophie wasn't surprised – this was bad timing.

She tiptoed closer to the door.

'Yes,' Mr Clarke went on. 'You see, witches have

been involved in Turlingham since the school was first built, and we would very much like to celebrate our heritage with a gathering in the magical library.'

'What an excellent idea!' Sophie's dad exclaimed. Then he added, 'But of course it's up to you, darling.'

Sophie's mum took a moment to reply. 'Well, I ... I don't quite know. How would it work? Would you need any, er, special, er, magical arrangements?'

'No, not at all.' Mr Clarke sounded eager. 'We would do all the organising. Your guests wouldn't know anything was going on.'

'You want to hold it on the same night as our anniversary party?' Sophie's mum said doubtfully.

'Yes, on Founder's Night. It's important to have it on the exact date – Benedict Wapentake is one of our greatest heroes.'

There was a long pause. Even though Sophie couldn't actually see her, she could just tell that her mum had her eyes closed, trying to think this through carefully.

'Tamsin,' said Sophie's dad, 'you know it's essential for Sophie to find out more about her heritage.'

'I suppose so . . . ' Sophie's mum sighed.

Sophie held her breath, hoping she would say yes.

'And I will help arrange it,' her dad added. 'I'll make sure the rest of the school isn't aware of it at all.'

Another long pause. Then, 'Very well,' said her mum. 'As long as the school isn't disturbed in the process, I don't see any harm in it.'

Sophie squealed with excitement before she knew what she was doing – then clapped a hand over her mouth.

'Sophie?' her mum said.

Her dad laughed. Sophie jumped back as he opened the door, grinning. Behind him, her mum tried to look stern, but had to smile. 'Come on in then,' she said. 'I suppose you're not that tired after all!'

Sophie sidled in, blushing. 'I'm sorry. I know I shouldn't have listened,' she said, hanging her head. 'But this is so exciting! I'm going to have two parties to go to in one night!'

Mrs Clarke gave a laugh and Mr Clarke bared his teeth in a smile.

'Thank you so much for thinking up the idea,'

Sophie said to Mr and Mrs Clarke. 'I'd be happy to help in any way.'

'That's very sweet of you, dear.' Mrs Clarke stood up. 'For now, though, we've taken up enough of your time.'

She reached out to shake Sophie's mum's hand, then seemed to change her mind and awkwardly moved forward to hug her instead. 'Thank you so much for your decision,' she said, looking into her eyes. 'Family and heritage are so important, don't you think?'

'Yes, of course.' Sophie's mum smoothed her hair as Mr Clarke and Sophie's dad shook hands.

Sophie followed her mum and the Clarkes to the door.

'Oh, your coats—' Sophie's dad went to fetch them.

As they waited for him to return Mr Clarke said abruptly, 'I was so sorry about the time capsule being stolen. Do the police have any leads?'

Sophie's mum looked puzzled. 'How did you know? I was just drafting the letter to parents now ... Oh, I suppose Abbie must have told you.'

'Yes,' said Mrs Clarke, just as Mr Clarke said, 'No.'

Sophie stared at them, suddenly even more awake than before. Mr Clarke cleared his throat. 'Abbie mentioned something about it, in passing, when she called me earlier.'

That's weird, thought Sophie. Had Abbie mentioned it or not?

Sophie's mum frowned, obviously suspicious too, but at that moment Sophie's dad came back, loaded with the Clarkes' coats. 'Well, it was good to see you,' he said, shaking their hands again as he handed out coats and gloves and hats. 'Don't be strangers. Drop round any time you like!'

'Oh, we will. Thank you so much. Goodbye!' Mr Clarke seemed hugely relieved. As soon as he was bundled up he hurried out of the door, and his wife followed him.

'Now Sophie,' said her mum sternly as soon as the door was closed. 'Bed!' She pointed up the stairs and Sophie ran up them.

The Clarkes were up to something and she wanted to know what it was. They showed up the moment the time capsule did. Then it went missing on Abbie's first night at the school. The Clarkes had known the time capsule was stolen, but how? Their explanation didn't convince her.

Instead of getting into bed Sophie got dressed in the same dark clothes she had worn the night before. She texted Katy in the dark: THINK MR AND MRS CLARKE ARE INVOLVED IN THE MISSING CAPSULE. MEET YOU UNDER THE OLD OAK IN 5 SO WE CAN FOLLOW THEM.

She glanced out of the window. A tall figure and a short one were making their way, not towards the car park, but towards the lighthouse.

She didn't know if she had Katy's way of sensing things, but she could certainly identify a lie when she heard one.

TEN

As Sophie crossed the courtyard she saw Katy standing in the shadows under the oak tree. She quickened her pace, Gally sprinting along beside her. Frost glittered on the ground and the wind stirred the dead leaves across the stone flags.

Katy was wearing black too, and bouncing on her tiptoes to keep warm. 'I knew there was something weird about Abbie,' she greeted Sophie in a whisper.

'Well, I don't know about Abbie, just her parents,' Sophie whispered back. 'But if you're right . . . '

Katy raised an eyebrow at her.

' . . . I'll let you do the biggest, fattest "I told you so" dance ever seen.'

Katy snorted a giggle. 'Hold you to that,' she whispered. Then she grabbed Sophie's arm and pointed.

A shaft of moonlight caught Mr and Mrs Clarke creeping along by the clifftop fence as if they were trying not to be seen.

Sophie followed them, Katy at her heels. The Clarkes edged along the fence, then paused in the shadow of the lighthouse. Sophie heard a clip and a ping. It sounded as if the Clarkes had used wire cutters. A second later she saw Mr Clarke bend the fence back and Mrs Clarke squeezed through the gap. Mr Clarke followed with a little more difficulty.

Sophie exchanged a glance with Katy. *Definitely* up to something!

They got as close as they dared – just in time to see the lighthouse door open. It was impossible to make out who was in the darkness inside, but the Clarkes hurried in and the door shut behind them.

Sophie and Katy ducked through the gap in the

fence and raced to the lighthouse door. Sophie pushed it ajar and peered inside. Above them the Clarkes' footsteps shuffled on the stone stairs, and torchbeams wavered across the curved walls. Finally there was the sound of a door creaking open and then shut.

'They've gone into the lantern room!' Katy whispered. Sophie nodded. Breaking into the lighthouse didn't mean the Clarkes had the time capsule, but if not, what *were* they up to?

Sophie put Gally in her pocket and tiptoed up the winding stairs, Katy close behind her. It was icy cold and the wind outside sounded like a desperate beast trying to get in. She finally reached the door of the lantern room, and pushed it gingerly open just a crack.

The room blazed with light – but not from the old lantern itself, which stood dark at the centre of the room. Hundreds of candles had been placed around, on the floor and the windowsills, and their light glittered from the storm panes to all sides. Someone was lighting the last of the candles, someone with deep red hair pulled into a ponytail.

Abbie.

Sophie felt Katy nudging her arm and turned round. Katy stuck her fingers in her ears, crossed her eyes, stuck her tongue out and jiggled around on the spot. Sophie pinched her nose to stop a giggle bursting out: it was clearly the biggest, fattest 'I told you so' dance she'd ever seen.

Abbie blew out the match and turned to her parents, who were hunched over something placed on a rickety table by the window. 'That's the last one, Dad,' she said.

'Excellent.' Mr Clarke straightened up and Sophie saw what was on the table. The time capsule.

Why had they taken it? What were they going to do now? Maybe she should run back to her parents and get them to phone the police. But then Mr Clarke picked up something large and heavy-looking from the table. It was a book with a cracked leather cover and faded gold symbols marked on it.

Mr Clarke took a deep breath and looked at his wife and daughter. Sophie could see the thin sweat on his forehead in the moonlight.

'Join the circle,' he said.

Mrs Clarke and Abbie stepped forwards. Abbie looked nervous. Mrs Clarke reached out and took her hand. Mr Clarke opened the book and began to read.

'Powers of the Earth,' he began. 'Earth, fire, water and wind ... '

Mrs Clarke and Abbie joined in, echoing his words. Katy tugged Sophie's arm.

'They're casting a spell!' she whispered. 'We've got to stop them, quick!'

Sophie knew Katy was right. She didn't know what spell the Clarkes were casting, but they were thieves so there was every chance it might be an evil one. It wasn't worth the risk. There was no time to lose.

She flung the door open. They all turned to her as she rushed in and knocked the book out of Mr Clarke's hands. It crashed to the floor.

Mr Clarke jumped, Mrs Clarke shrieked and Abbie gasped out: 'Sophie! Katy!' She looked back and forth between them. 'What are you doing here?'

Sophie clenched her fists to stop herself trembling. 'I think we should be asking *you* that,' she said. 'I don't know what you're up to, but that,' she pointed at the time capsule, 'isn't yours. I want an explanation, or I'm calling my dad.'

Mr and Mrs Clarke looked at each other.

'Tell them, Andrew,' Mrs Clarke said, her voice shaking.

Mr Clarke looked back at Sophie. 'I'm so sorry, Sophie.' He sounded sad and embarrassed. 'I didn't want anyone outside our family to find out, but now that you have ... You see, although the capsule does not belong to us, what is inside does.'

Katy muttered something under her breath. She didn't sound convinced.

'We have known for a long time,' he continued, 'that the spirit of one of our ancestors—'

'Bethan Clarke,' Abbie interrupted. She sounded more serious than Sophie had ever heard her.

'Yes, Bethan,' he continued. 'Her spirit is trapped in this capsule.'

Sophie drew a breath of amazement. She looked at the squat metal box – the squat metal prison – on the table.

'We Clarkes have been waiting three hundred years

to have the chance to finally release her spirit and send it to its rest.'

'But how did it happen?' Sophie said. It was a horrible thought – the poor woman's ghost, trapped and alone for three hundred years.

Mr Clarke coughed, sounding embarrassed. He gave a sideways glance at Katy. 'It was a witch hunter who imprisoned her,' he said. 'A Gibson witch hunter.'

Katy blushed. 'I'm so, so sorry! I can't even—'

Mr Clarke put his hand up then hurried on. 'That's all ancient history now. We don't want revenge.' He looked so sincere. 'But we *do* want to free poor Bethan.'

Sophie was stunned. She turned to Abbie. 'So you planned this all along? Does this mean that night when we all went down to see it and found it missing, you'd already been there and stolen it? You were pretending the whole time?' It was hard to even say the words. 'I trusted you!'

Abbie looked at her pleadingly. 'I'm sorry, Sophie. I didn't want to lie to you, but I had to for the sake of my family. Please say you understand why I did it.'

Sophie swallowed and nodded. She *did* understand – even though she couldn't help feeling betrayed. It wasn't Abbie's fault. She'd done what she had to do.

'That's OK,' she said. She forced a smile. 'I understand how important family is.'

Katy nodded. 'So do I. If it was one of my family trapped in there . . . I'd have done the same.'

Abbie smiled gratefully.

'Thank you so much for being understanding,' said Mrs Clarke softly.

Sophie looked back at the spell book that lay on the floor and watched as Mr Clarke bent to pick it up. Mrs Clarke stretched out her hands. 'Would you like to join us, Sophie?'

Sophie wasn't sure. Her mum had said no magic, but this was an emergency. If the Clarkes were right, their ancestor had been trapped in this box for 300 years. She deserved to be released and put at peace.

'Yes,' she said, finally. 'The more witches the better, right?'

Sophie and Abbie walked forward. They formed a

circle, hand in hand. Mr Clarke reopened the book and cleared his throat.

Katy, looking a little embarrassed, moved away, but Mrs Clarke smiled at her across the circle.

'Don't go too far, Katy. Now you're here, it's right that you should be present. This is part of your story too.'

Mr Clarke began to chant once more. 'As the thunder breaks the night, let our spell break these bonds. As the lightning splits the tree, let our spell split this prison. As the waves crack the cliff, let our spell crack your chains.' His voice grew louder and more forceful, like a storm growing in strength. 'Be free, Bethan! Be free!'

Sophie felt power humming through her hands, as if the four of them were an electrical circuit. She couldn't tell if she was tingling with excitement or magic. This was the strongest spell she had ever been part of! Above the lighthouse she heard the rumble of gathering thunder.

Abbie's hand tightened on hers.

Mr Clarke chanted on, his voice mingling with the thunder. 'Open! Open! Open!'

Through the opposite windows Sophie could see the dark clouds massing and boiling in a storm that seemed to have the lighthouse as its centre.

'Open!' Mr Clarke repeated.

Mrs Clarke echoed him: 'Open!'

And Abbie, her voice trembling, echoed: 'Open!'

'Open!' Sophie cried.

Thunder clapped almost above them. There was a blinding flash of white light. Sophie gasped. When she could see again the time capsule was open, the lock melted, twisted and smoking.

'We did it!' Abbie exclaimed, letting go of Sophie's hand.

Sophie breathed out.

'Wow,' Katy said from the door.

Mr Clarke put the book down.

'Bethan?' he said, his voice trembling. 'Bethan, it's us. Your family.'

As the rain lessened and the storm moved away, Sophie realised that a soft hissing noise, like escaping gas, was coming from the time capsule, and it was getting louder. She leaned forward to look inside.

She saw a small silver coil, shiny as mercury, at the bottom of the box. It writhed and slithered like a snake. It was growing, fast.

Sophie jumped back just in time. The coil surged, hissing, out of the capsule like a cloud of silver steam. At one moment it looked like a snake with angry, bared jaws, then it looked like a woman with long, floating silver tendrils of hair. The snake and the woman seemed meshed together, hissing furiously.

Mrs Clarke raised a trembling hand to the ghost. 'Bethan, is that you?'

'It *is* her. The snake was her familiar!' Mr Clarke said triumphantly. 'Bethan, we are so glad to have freed you!'

The ghost gazed at him. Sophie shuddered at the look on her half-woman, half-snake face. She drew back sharply, then lunged at Mrs Clarke with a terrible hiss. Mrs Clarke screamed and ducked.

'Free! Free at last!' Bethan screamed. She swept over their heads and flew around the room like a silver tornado, the candles blowing out as she passed, wild laughter echoing. The candles clattered to the ground, and Bethan swooped in among them, flinging them around the room. Sophie ducked as a brass candlestick hurtled towards her.

Bethan was free all right, but she wasn't happy!

Mr Clarke straightened up, the spell book held above his head in defence.

'Bethan!' Mr Clarke shouted. 'Stop this! We're your family. We've come to help you—'

'Free! Free for ever, free at last!' Bethan dashed at him, flicking her tail to pelt him with candles. Mr Clarke dodged behind the lantern again, but Bethan snatched his glasses from his face and flung them across the room. The book followed, pages flapping, right at Katy, who dodged it.

Bethan stopped dead. She stared at Katy, her tongue flickering out of her mouth.

'Fee, fi, fo, fum!' she hissed. Malice blazed from her like heat from a fire. 'I smell the blood of a Gibson!'

Sophie stood in front of Katy to protect her.

'*Your* family locked me up!' Bethan yelled.

She hurtled at Katy, knocking Sophie to one side so she stumbled to the floor. Katy screamed and tried to hide behind the lantern, but Bethan flew round and round her, faster and faster.

'Katy!' Sophie tried to reach her, but Bethan's force threw her back.

'Help!' Katy screamed. 'It hurts! Stop her!'

'Years – decades – of loneliness and torture! Centuries! I'll have my revenge!' Bethan's voice was like whirling silver blades.

'Stop her! Make her stop! She's hurting Katy!' Sophie screamed at Mr Clarke.

'B-b-but how?' Mr Clarke peered out from behind the door.

Sophie looked desperately around and saw the book, spread-eagled on the floor. She grabbed it and threw it to Mr Clarke.

The only way to stop Bethan was to put her spirit at peace, making her disappear for ever. 'Finish the spell!'

Mr Clarke fumbled a catch and, holding the book close to his face, flipped through the pages. He turned the pages again and again, backwards and forwards, a look of growing panic on his face.

Katy screamed louder. Sophie tried to reach her again, but it was like trying to walk through a tornado.

'Hurry!' she shouted to Mr Clarke.

'It's gone,' Mr Clarke blurted. 'The rest of the spell is missing!' He lifted up the book to show the ragged edge where a clump of pages had been ripped out.

'What?' Mrs Clarke peered out, horrified, from behind the table. 'Where is it?' She began searching around on the floor. Mr Clarke joined her. Abbie was flattened against the windows, a look of terror on her face.

There wasn't a second to lose. If they couldn't save Katy, Sophie would have to do it herself. She forced her way through the wailing, screaming wind and hugged Katy tight, then lifted up her wrist so that the friendship bracelet on it showed.

'You might be a ghost, Bethan, but you're still a witch. You know what the gold in this bracelet means – you can't hurt her!' she shouted. 'Go away and leave us alone!'

Bethan's wild laughter echoed from all sides. 'Oh, I'll go! But I'll be back. And I'll have my revenge!'

She swooped away from them with a last wild yelp. The window trembled as she shot through it. Her curses and wailing dwindled into the distance and she shrank with them until she was gone completely.

In the silence, Katy's sobs died down as Sophie hugged her.

'It's OK. You're safe now. She's gone.' Sophie stroked Katy's hair.

Katy pulled herself upright and dried her eyes. 'Gone ... but for how long?' She bit her lip.

Sophie looked around at the Clarkes' pale, shocked faces. Katy was right. Thanks to them, Turlingham was now haunted. And this ghost was out to get her best friend!

ELEVEN

Sophie sat in the hall with her friends, trying hard to concentrate on Mark's singing as she listened to him audition for the boy's part in the duet. She shifted on her chair. It wasn't easy, when she didn't know where Bethan was, or when she might strike . . .

Kaz nudged Sophie, who flinched. 'Check out Mrs Richardson,' Kaz whispered.

Mrs Richardson was trying not to wince as she played along on the piano – Mark's voice wasn't much better than Abbie's.

Just as Sophie thought that, a distant, angry wailing echoed through the hall. Her friends looked up in surprise, then started giggling. Mrs Richardson looked annoyed and played louder. Mark sang louder too. Which didn't help.

'Thank you, Mark, that was a very good effort,' Mrs Richardson said as he came to the end of the song. Mark's face fell. She frowned into the audience. 'And I hope it wasn't one of you making that dreadful noise. It isn't kind to mock.'

'No, but it *was* quite funny!' Kaz whispered again as Mark came down from the stage and Callum went up. Everyone except Sophie, Katy and Abbie sniggered. 'I wonder who it was? One of the Year Eights?'

Sophie caught Katy's eye. Maybe . . . and maybe it was Bethan.

'That's enough gossiping.' Mrs Richardson sounded cross, and Sophie hastily straightened up and looked to the stage. 'Callum, please begin.'

As soon as Callum started singing Sophie knew he was the best of the lot. She glanced around at the others to share her opinion. They all smiled back at her, except for Katy, who beamed at Callum with eyes for no one else.

'Brilliant!' Mrs Richardson exclaimed as Callum came to the end. 'Well, I think we have our male singer. Thank you, Callum.'

Callum grinned and headed back to the seats. Sophie and the others whistled and clapped. Callum, blushing, went down the row of chairs and took his seat next to Katy. Katy squeezed his arm.

'Now, let's move on to the girls.' Mrs Richardson looked towards the Year 9 girls. 'Who's willing to have a go?'

Erin and Kaz suddenly became very interested in looking at their shoes. Lauren and Joanna stared out of the window. They weren't going to audition if Callum was the male lead – Katy had to get the part.

Sophie nudged Katy. 'Go on!' she whispered.

Katy shyly put her hand up. Only four other girls joined her.

Mrs Richardson frowned. 'No more? Are you sure? Sophie? No? Erin ...? Well ... never mind, let's get started.'

One by one, the girls went up. Sophie listened anxiously. She so wanted Katy to be the best. She wished she could use magic to help her win, but even if her mum hadn't forbidden it, it would have been too much like cheating.

'Very good, Claire. Thank you.' Mrs Richardson smiled to the girl who'd just auditioned, then looked up towards the benches. 'Katy, you're next, I think.'

As Katy stood up she clenched her teeth.

Abbie touched her arm. 'Katy, have some of this.' She held up a bottle of water to her. 'It'll stop dry mouth.'

Katy's hands shook a little as she took the bottle and drank. She gave it back to Abbie and went up to Mrs Richardson. Sophie crossed her fingers for luck.

'One, two, three . . . ' Mrs Richardson began playing.

As the intro ended, Katy opened her mouth to sing . . . but no sound came out.

Katy looked horrified. Her mouth opened and closed soundlessly.

Mrs Richardson stopped playing. 'Let's try that again, shall we?' she said.

Sophie watched in disbelief as Katy turned red in

the face. She was clearly *trying* to sing – but all that came out were croaking noises. She sounded like a frog. Sophie could see tears in Katy's eyes. Some of the boys at the back were laughing.

'What's going on?' Erin whispered, looking anxious.

Sophie shook her head. She had no idea. Normally, Katy had a great voice.

Mrs Richardson stopped playing and stood up. Katy was clutching her throat, looking shocked.

Mrs Richardson went to her and put a sympathetic hand on her shoulder. 'I'm sorry, dear. You obviously have a . . . very sore throat. There will be a lot of practice between now and the concert, so I don't think it's your moment, I'm afraid. See the school nurse and she'll give you something for your throat.'

Katy nodded silently. She hurried back down the stairs. Sophie and the others made way for her as she sidled back along the row and the next girl took her place.

'Katy, what happened?' Callum whispered, as Sophie hugged her.

Katy shook her head. Her eyes were filled with tears.

'I d-don't know. My voice just wasn't there.'

'But it is now,' Sophie said, staring at her.

Katy put a hand to her neck. 'I don't even have a sore throat. It's so strange . . . ' She fell silent as the last girl ended her song.

Could it be Bethan at work? But it was a petty revenge, if it was. This didn't seem like her, somehow. 'Nerves do funny things to people sometimes,' said Sophie.

'So if that's all the girls who want to audition,' Mrs Richardson began, closing the piano lid, 'I think—'

'Mrs Richardson,' came Abbie's voice. 'I'd like to give it a go. If that's OK.'

Sophie cringed. Erin pulled a worried face. They all knew that Abbie wasn't the best singer. Sophie hoped she wasn't about to seriously embarrass herself.

'Really?' Mrs Richardson didn't look hopeful, but she nodded. 'Come on up then.'

Abbie took a sip from her bottle of water and joined Mrs Richardson on stage.

Good luck, Abbie, thought Sophie. And she crossed her fingers again.

Except that when Abbie actually started singing . . . she was brilliant!

Sophie glanced round at her friends – who all looked as astonished as she felt – then back at Abbie. Abbie had a smug smile on her face. A beautiful, melodic and perfectly pitched voice floated from her mouth, sweet and clear and strong. Despite herself, Sophie felt the hairs on the back of her neck prickle. By the look on Mrs Richardson's face, she couldn't believe her luck.

'Well, that's quite conclusive!' she said, before the last bar of music had even died away. 'Abbie, the part is yours. I must say I had no idea you sang so well.'

Neither had we! thought Sophie. She glanced around at her friends. Katy looked stunned, Kaz and Erin disbelieving. Joanna and Lauren were wide-eyed. Callum didn't look at all pleased at the prospect of singing with Abbie ... and Sophie wasn't sure she blamed him. That voice was too good to be true. Abbie was up to something!

The bell for the end of school rang, and everyone headed for the door. Sophie made her way through the crowd to Abbie, who was putting her bottle of water away. Sophie tried to get a good look at it. It *looked* like ordinary water.

'Abbie, you ... you didn't use magic to give yourself a good voice, did you?' she said.

Abbie widened her eyes and tucked a lock of hair behind her ear. 'No, of course not! I just practised, that's all.' She shrugged. 'I'm sorry about Katy. I wouldn't have auditioned if she had a chance, but since she's lost her voice ... ' Abbie didn't *look* sorry. 'Well, I just love singing duets!'

Sophie frowned. She was about to ask if she could have some of Abbie's water – if Abbie refused, she could be pretty sure it was enchanted – when Mrs Richardson came over with Callum.

'Abbie, you can stay behind with Callum and practise with me now,' she said. 'There'll be a lot of practice, so I hope you like each other's company!'

Abbie beamed. 'We *love* each other's company, Mrs Richardson!' She slipped her arm into Callum's and led him off to the piano. Callum went, glancing mournfully over his shoulder at Katy.

Sophie saw Katy standing alone, looking miserable

as the rest of the students poured out of the doors, talking and laughing. She wound her way through the rows of chairs to join her. Erin, Kaz, Lauren and Joanna were right behind.

'I can't believe that!' said Erin.

'What is Abbie playing at?' said Kaz.

Katy was seething. 'She stole my voice and now she's stealing my boyfriend!' She angrily swung her bag on to her shoulder.

Sophie paused. Could Abbie's mysterious water bottle have sabotaged Katy's voice as well? She didn't want to believe Abbie would be *that* cruel. But even if she was, Sophie was certain that Callum wouldn't let himself be stolen. 'Oh, but—' Sophie began.

'Don't you dare!' Katy interrupted her, eyes flashing with anger.

'What?' Katy had never spoken to Sophie liked this.

'Don't you dare stick up for *her*!'

'I wasn't,' said Sophie. She could feel herself getting hot.

'Whatever! It's been "Abbie this, Abbie that" ever since she arrived!' She stormed from the hall.

From the looks on her friends' faces, it seemed they all agreed with Katy. Even worse, Sophie suspected they were right. She had been putting Abbie above everything, even her best friend. She felt terrible.

'Come on,' said Erin. 'Let's go after her.'

'Wait.' Sophie held up her hands to stop them following Katy. 'Let me go first,' she said. 'I want to apologise.'

The others hung back as Sophie shouted, 'Katy!' She ran after her, out into the corridor, but she was too late. The corridors were filled with people pouring out of lessons, and Katy was nowhere to be seen.

Sophie looked for her everywhere she could think of – the dorms, the dining room, the tuck shop, the toilets, the nurse's room, even into the empty classrooms. She couldn't find her anywhere.

After almost an hour she went outside. There was a bonfire on the other side of the courtyard. A group were gathered around it. She heard Erin's voice and ran towards them, crisp leaves crunching under her feet.

'Now I've told you lot before, keep back,' Mr Jones,

the caretaker, was saying as Sophie reached them. He shovelled more leaves on to the fire, making it very smoky. The flames danced and leapt as Mr Jones picked up his wheelbarrow and trundled it away to fetch another heap of leaves.

'Have you seen Katy?' Sophie said to the others.

'You didn't catch up with her?' asked Lauren.

Sophie shook her head miserably. 'I can't find her anywhere.'

'I'm sure she's all right,' said Joanna. 'Maybe she just wants some space.'

'Maybe the poltergeist got her,' Mark said with a laugh, his arms around Erin.

Sophie looked at him sharply. 'Poltergeist?'

'Yeah, didn't you hear? A shelf nearly fell on Ashton Gibson in Art class this morning. At least we think it fell ... it might have been pushed. Woooooooo!' He made a ghost noise and everyone laughed with him.

The others laughed, but all Sophie could think about was poor Ashton. Of course, as a Gibson, Bethan was out to get him too, and he had no idea.

'Did anything happen to anyone else?' asked Sophie.

'Well, there was that awful wailing in choir practice.' Kaz giggled. 'Mark, your voice clearly raised the dead!'

'Don't joke.' Lauren's voice shook. 'I'm scared of ghosts.'

'Oh come on, Lauren, it's not real,' Kaz said, putting an arm around her. 'It's just someone playing a prank.'

Sophie was almost sure that it *wasn't* a prank, not with Bethan on the loose. She opened her mouth to tell the others to be careful, when she heard, through the crackle of the bonfire, a strange creaking, groaning noise. She looked up – just in time to see a branch of the tree sag towards them.

'Look out!' she exclaimed. She jumped back, pushing Lauren away as she did so. Lauren stumbled towards the bonfire. The others scattered and the branch crashed down in between Lauren and Sophie. They stared at it in shock.

'I *told* you there was a poltergeist!' Mark laughed, but his voice sounded shaky. Everyone else giggled nervously.

'Don't laugh!' Lauren was almost crying; she

hugged herself and backed away even closer to the bonfire. 'You'll make it angry!'

That made the boys laugh harder. Sophie was about to tell them to stop, but before she had taken two steps there was a sudden gust of wind from the other direction. The flames of the bonfire flapped like a golden flag, and for a second Sophie thought she saw an angry, fanged face in it, hissing smoke. A forked tongue of fire licked out like a whip and caught Lauren's glove.

'Lauren!' Sophie screamed. 'Your glove! It's on fire!'

TWELVE

Sophie ran towards Lauren as she cried out in fear. Lauren tried to pat out the flame on her glove, but all that happened was that her other glove caught fire too.

'Help! Help me, it hurts!' She tugged at her gloves.

The fire was catching too easily. This flame was magic. Sophie was about to try and cast a spell, but Mr Jones was already there. He pushed her out of the way and wrapped Lauren's hands in a fire blanket.

Lauren collapsed to the ground, sobbing.

'Oh my gosh!' Erin started forward to give her a hug, but Mr Jones put out a hand to keep her back.

'Gently, give her some air.' The fire was out but Lauren was still sobbing. Mr Jones looked panicked. 'I told you lot to stay away from the bonfire!'

'We were!' Joanna protested.

'Honestly, we were, Mr Jones,' Oliver said. 'That flame just came out of nowhere.'

'Well, never mind that now. She's had a shock and she's burned. I'd best put this out – can you get her to the nurse?'

'I'll go,' said Sophie, and everyone echoed her. 'We'll all go.'

Joanna took Lauren's arm and they all hurried off to the nurse's station. As they crossed the courtyard Sophie realised there was someone following them. She turned round. It was Ashton.

She dropped back and went to him.

'I saw what happened,' he said in a low voice as she reached him. 'It's magic, isn't it?'

Sophie nodded.

'I could tell when the shelf fell on me. Everyone said it must have broken, but I checked and it had unscrewed itself from the wall. Something around here doesn't like us.'

'I know what it is . . . ' She quickly told him what she and Katy had discovered. 'So now Bethan's loose, and very angry – and I'm sure she's taking revenge on anyone she can. I'm so sorry, Ashton, we should have told you earlier.'

'Is Katy OK?' Ashton seemed more worried for his sister than for himself.

Sophie nodded. 'She's fine. But you both have to watch out. Whatever Bethan was like when she was alive, being locked up in a box for three hundred years has driven her crazy. I know it sounds cruel, but we've got to capture her again. Just until we can find the missing spell that would put her spirit to rest.'

Ashton nodded, jamming his hands deeper into his coat pockets. 'You're right. But how do we do it?'

Sophie thought about it for a moment. 'I don't know,' she said as the idea formed in her head, 'but maybe a combination of witch and witch hunter magic could be strong enough to do it.' She glanced at him for his reaction.

Ashton nodded. 'Sounds as if it would work. Witch magic could summon Bethan and then witch hunter magic could enchant a container to lock her in. Just until we can put her to rest.'

Sophie felt hopeful. This felt like a real plan.

Ashton was reaching for his phone. 'I'll call Katy. Then you two can get to work.'

Sophie touched his arm to stop him dialling. 'Katy's not my biggest fan right now. I thought ... I wondered ...' she found herself blushing, '... maybe *you* could try a spell with me?'

Ashton's eyes widened in surprise, then he smiled. 'I'd love to!' He checked his watch. 'Let's do it now. I'll get a container and meet you in one of the music practice rooms in ten.'

'And I'll try and find a spell for summoning. There might be one in the library, or my dad's shed,' Sophie said.

Ashton grinned. 'Deal!'

He turned and ran towards the Science lab. Sophie

stood for a second, watching him run. Her cheeks were burning. She was about to do a spell with Ashton ... and she couldn't wait!

Sophie walked nervously down the music corridor, past the practice rooms and the sound of people playing piano scales and squeaking through cello pieces. Her stomach was churning, and she didn't think it was just because she was about to try something that could be dangerous. Casting a spell with Ashton was ... well, it was going to be interesting!

She glanced into each practice room as she passed. Ashton was in the last one. He was playing the piano. The hair on the back of Sophie's neck stood up as beautiful waves of music came to her through the door. He looked so engrossed, his dark hair flopping over his eyes.

He came to the end of the piece, and she opened the door and went in. Ashton started, looking embarrassed. 'Sorry.' He jumped up.

'You're brilliant!' Sophie said, and she meant it. 'Why don't you do piano lessons?'

Ashton shrugged. 'Oh, it's a waste of time. I should be studying witch hunter stuff.' He looked at the floor.

'Is that what you think, or what your parents think?'

Ashton didn't say anything. Sophie could see he didn't like talking about it.

He reached for the big glass jar on top of the piano. 'I brought this from the Science lab. I think if I add certain ingredients when Bethan is present, and do an entrapment chant, it should pull her in and keep her there.'

Sophie nodded. 'And I think I can summon her using these.' She put down the book she had brought from her dad's shed: *The Realm of Spirit.* Beside the book she laid down three plants: convolvulus, mandrake root, and a single four-leaved clover. 'At least, I hope so . . . I've never tried summoning before.'

She opened the book to the summoning spell, looked at Ashton and took a deep breath. Her heart was beating fast and she could see his eyes were shining with excitement. 'So . . . are we ready?' she said.

Ashton nodded. He looked nervous too, but there was a splinter of excitement glowing in his eyes. 'Bring it on!' he said.

As Sophie rubbed the three herbs together in her hands, murmuring the words of power, Ashton added pinches of strong-smelling powder to the jar, and dropped in what looked like a single pearl. The pearl popped like a soap bubble, and there was a faint, distant sound, like bells chiming. The powders in the jar mixed and turned into black smoke that billowed out into the room.

Sophie held her breath, but Ashton shook his head. 'It's all right – you should be able to breathe through it.'

Sophie tried it, and found that he was right. Soon the room was so dark that Sophie could see nothing at all except the glowing jar.

'Perhaps we should hold hands,' Ashton said, then blushed. 'You know, to make it more powerful.'

Sophie took his hand. It felt warm. She tried to concentrate as she said, 'Forces of the Earth. Earth, water, wind and fire.' Her Source glowed and a tingle spread all the way up her arms. 'Use your great strength to draw the spirit of Bethan Clarke to me. Whether she be hidden in water, earth, wind or fire – find her and summon her!'

Nothing happened. She and Ashton shared an awkward look.

Then she heard a wailing, howling noise, just like the one she had heard in the auditions, and squeezed Ashton's hand tighter.

'Is this a bit crazy?' she whispered, trying to keep her tone light. 'Actually *summoning* a ghostly, angry witch?'

Ashton's voice was tense. 'Too late now . . . '

The wailing grew louder and more furious, and a small silver dot, like a coin, formed over the jar.

'Earth, water, wind and fire,' Sophie repeated over and over again. The silver dot grew and grew and she could see that it was Bethan. She looked like a serpent with a woman's head. Her eyes were tortured, furious and flashing silver. She grew until she towered over them, her body like a huge cloud, dotted with silver flashes like lightning. She opened her mouth, revealing fangs like a snake, and gave a loud, vicious hiss.

Sophie was shaking inside and out, but she stood firm. 'Bethan,' she said, 'I'm sorry, but you're hurting people.'

Bethan hissed again. It sounded like she was laughing at them.

'We're going to imprison you again, but only for a short while. Only until we can find out how to put your spirit to rest.'

'Rest?' Bethan cackled out a laugh. Her tongue flickered silver. 'Rest? You fool, I don't want to rest. I'm having too much fun!'

She lashed out with a coil of her cloudy body and tried to knock the jar off the piano. Ashton caught it and held it tightly.

'*Continens pro quod continentur. Incarcerare! Incarcerare!*' he said in a powerful voice.

Bethan hissed and laughed.

'Stupid Gibson! Your powers are useless!' She swooped at him again. Ashton ducked behind the piano.

'*Incarcerare! Incarcerare!*' he shouted.

Bethan thrashed like she was struggling against some invisible ropes.

'Keep going, Ashton!' Sophie shouted. She clenched her fists desperately – this had to work!

'*Incarcerare!*' Ashton went on. He held the jar up high into the air. 'Bethan Clarke, you cannot withstand my powers! Witch, enter the vessel!'

Bethan howled and hissed and writhed. A sound like thunder came from the coils of her body. Sophie whooped as she saw the witch being dragged slowly but surely towards the glass jar. The dark clouds began to turn purple as Bethan was stuffed into the container. The jar filled with silver coils. The spell was working!

But just as Ashton was going to slam the lid on to the jar, a silver light bathed the room. Sophie saw Bethan hesitate, a puzzled, startled look on her face.

Sophie's heart sank – was the spell not working after all? But then, with a last shuddering cry, Bethan vanished. Her voice faded away and the clouds of black smoke cleared.

Ashton straightened up, still holding the jar – which was empty. He wiped the smoke smuts from his face. 'What happened there? I thought she was going to end up in the jar.'

Sophie looked around her, confused. Bethan certainly wasn't here any more, she could sense it. The prickly, tense fear that she had had for so long had gone. And that was the important thing.

'I don't know ... but she's gone all right!' She turned to Ashton. 'We did it!' She forced excitement into her voice. 'Woo hoo!'

Without thinking, she reached out to hug him. Ashton's warm arms went around her. His lips brushed her cheek, then, as she turned towards him, her lips. Sophie's heart pounded and she tingled with a feeling that wasn't just magic or adrenalin. Should she pull back? Or should she— But at that second the supper bell drilled through the air. She jolted back, startled, and shyly smiled at Ashton, who blushed and smiled back.

Crazy ghost witches she could deal with. But these feelings she was getting for Ashton were a whole different story! And scarier than anything.

THIRTEEN

Sophie was curled up in front of the television, watching her favourite soap. The fire was on, she could smell something delicious cooking in the oven, and outside rain was lashing down against the windows. She wriggled her toes, snuggling into the couch. Bethan was gone – not trapped in the jar, but gone for good. She'd told Abbie, who said her family were pleased they'd set Bethan free. Rosdet was home, dozing in front of the fire. And she'd nearly kissed Ashton.

If only Katy wasn't still angry with her, life would be pretty good.

The doorbell rang, and Sophie jumped up and ran to it. Outside stood Callum, shivering under an umbrella.

'Callum!' Sophie stood aside to let him in. 'Come in.'

Callum looked embarrassed as he shook the water from his umbrella into the porch. 'Thanks.'

Callum followed Sophie into the sitting room and stopped dead.

'Wow! Is that Rosdet?' he said, crouching for a closer look at the fox. 'I can't believe you've got a fox in your house. That's so cool!'

Rosdet opened one eye and closed it again.

'Does he get on with Gally?' Callum looked around as he sat down. 'Where *is* Gally?'

'I don't know.' Sophie frowned. 'I haven't seen him all evening. He usually curls up on my lap to watch TV.'

'Anyway, I need help,' said Callum, sitting down. 'I'm no good at girl stuff and I wondered if you could, um … you know, say something to her.'

'Katy? Because you know she's still not—'

Callum squirmed. 'No. Abbie.'

'Oh.'

'It was really awkward in the rehearsal.' Callum was blushing brighter and brighter red. 'I think she likes me. But I don't. Like her, that is. I like Katy. I really, really, really like Katy.'

'Right answer.' Sophie grinned at him. She was feeling worried though: it looked as if no one was going to get out of this situation without getting their feelings hurt. And as much as Abbie deserved it for going after a boy who already had a girlfriend, Sophie didn't like to see *anyone* get hurt.

'I tried to tell her that – you know, subtly,' Callum went on.

Sophie tried not to wince. Callum was about as subtle as Tabasco sauce in your eye.

'What happened? Was she really upset?'

'No,' said Callum. He sounded puzzled. 'That's the weird thing. She just said, "That's what you think," and walked off. Towards the Science lab. I mean, don't you think that's a bit weird?'

Sophie nodded. It *was* a bit weird.

'I thought you might tell her, you know, that she's really nice and everything but I just don't think of her like that. And can you say something to Katy for me too?' Callum scratched his ear, looking embarrassed. 'I think she might be angry with me. And I want her to know, you know, that there's no reason to be.'

Sophie sighed. 'She's angry with me too, so I'm not sure she'll listen. But I'll try.'

As she spoke there was a scratching at the door. Sophie went to open it and saw Gally sitting outside.

'There you are!' She bent to pick him up, but Gally jumped over her hands, his tail bristling.

Sophie watched in surprise as he scampered across the room, ducking in and out of the shadows, towards Rosdet. The fox uncurled and opened his eyes. Gally hissed angrily and swiped at him. Rosdet had to roll over fast to avoid being hit by his claws. He jumped up and growled at Gally.

'Gally!' Sophie exclaimed, shocked. She ran to pick him up, but Gally wriggled and hissed again, as if he wanted to get down and attack Rosdet. Rosdet backed away, still growling. 'What's got into you? I'm sorry, Rosdet.' Sophie had never seen Gally behave like that. 'Callum, why do you think he did that?' she said.

Callum cleared his throat. 'I don't know much about witches and familiars, but Gally's a squirrel, and Rosdet's, well, a fox,' he said. 'It's probably just nature.'

'I suppose,' said Sophie doubtfully. She stroked Gally's ears, trying to soothe him. 'But he's never been aggressive before. It just doesn't seem like him.'

There was a soft thump and she looked round to see that Mincing had come in and jumped on to the back of the couch. He was staring at Rosdet too, his ears laid flat and his fur bristling. Callum made a grab for him, but it was too late – Mincing leapt off the couch, claws out, and landed on Rosdet.

'Mincing! No!' Sophie exclaimed as the two animals locked in a hissing, growling, spitting ball of fur and teeth. They banged into a vase and it smashed on the hearthstone, dried flowers scattering. Gally gave a desperate twist and wriggle, jumped out of her hands and landed on the carpet. He dashed in to join the fight.

'Stop it! What are you doing? Stop!' Sophie shouted.

The fighting animals knocked into the lamp and Callum dived to catch it. Sophie edged around, trying to see a way to separate them, but it was impossible. They bumped into a bookcase, and books fell around them.

'What's going on?' Her mum ran in, followed by her dad. 'Oh my goodness!'

'Rosdet, stop this immediately! Mincing!' Sophie's dad strode across the room, picked up Rosdet by the scruff of his neck in one hand, and Mincing by the scruff of his neck in the other. The fox and the cat dangled, still growling at each other. They were covered in scratches and bites. Sophie swooped down and picked up Gally, who was trembling. His tail had been thoroughly gnawed.

'What on earth happened here?' Sophie's dad demanded to know.

'I don't know. Gally and Mincing just suddenly attacked Rosdet.' Sophie looked around at the mess the animals had made of the sitting room.

'Right, that's it.' Sophie's mum was breathing fast and her eyes were dangerously bright. 'I've had enough. The pair of you have turned my house into a zoo! From now on, no animals in the house.'

'But Tamsin—' Sophie's dad started.

'Squirrels and foxes should live outside,' said Sophie's mum.

'Oh Mum, no!' Sophie clutched Gally tight. 'It's cold out there!'

'Tamsin, that's not fair,' Sophie's dad said. 'They're familiars. You can't treat them like wild animals.'

'They're behaving exactly like wild animals! Look at the state of my sitting room – and my poor vase!'

'This is part of Sophie's heritage!' Sophie could hear her dad was angry too.

'Well, she can stay in touch with her heritage outside!' Sophie's mum was almost shouting.

Sophie backed to the door, and Callum followed her. They went into the hall and Sophie shut the door behind her. She could still hear her parents fighting, though. Witch hearing wasn't always a good thing.

Callum was frowning. 'You know, I noticed something odd about Rosdet,' he said. 'Do familiar foxes usually have purple eyes? I mean, Gally's eyes are normal.'

Sophie nodded. 'I asked my dad about that after we

got back. He says that strange things can happen to a familiar who's been mistreated.' She got her coat down from the hook. 'I'll walk with you some of the way. I want to go and see Katy tonight. Hopefully we can make up.'

It was bad enough that the familiars were fighting, *and* her parents were fighting, she didn't want to fight with Katy too. They had to sort this out.

Sophie walked along the Year 9 girls' corridor. There was still half an hour before lights-out and most of the girls were in the common room. The noise of laughter and talking and TV came from inside. Sophie glanced through the glass panel in the door but Katy wasn't with them. She walked on to Katy's dorm. Katy was lying on her bed, reading. She looked up as Sophie came through the door and immediately pushed the book under her pillow. Sophie just glimpsed some old, yellowed-looking pages.

Katy stared at Sophie.

Sophie smiled nervously. Katy's stare was unnerving, as if there was no expression at all in her eyes. 'Hi,' she said. 'What are you reading? Anything good?'

Katy's eyes flicked to the pillow. 'Nothing you'd be interested in,' she said.

Sophie shifted from foot to foot. It looked as if Katy was really angry with her. She seemed to be just waiting for her to go.

'I'm really sorry that I upset you,' she said. 'You were right. Abbie does like Callum. But Callum's not interested in her,' she added hurriedly. 'At all. You don't have to worry.'

Katy just looked back at her with the same flat, cold gaze.

Sophie felt Gally wriggling around in her bag.

'No, Gally,' she said to him. 'You're not coming out! You've caused enough trouble for one day!' She looked back at Katy. Maybe she was still worried about Bethan. She came forward and sat on the bed. 'And me and Ashton did a spell together.' She felt herself blushing and hurried on. 'I think we've managed to get rid of Bethan.'

Sophie was shocked by Katy's reaction: Katy laughed! A sharp, harsh cackle, completely unlike her normal laugh. She sat up, grinning, with a strange triumphant expression in her eyes. 'Do you really think a couple of kids could get rid of Bethan Clarke so easily?'

Sophie frowned. 'What?'

Katy gave a sudden, violent hiss and pushed Sophie hard. Sophie gasped as she slid off the bed and landed with a thump on the floor. Her face turned red and her eyes filled with tears as she looked up at Katy's grinning face.

She got to her feet, angry and hurt, leaving her bag where it had fallen.

'What's got into you, Katy? Why are you being like this?' She tried to catch Katy's eye, but her friend just shrugged and looked away.

Sophie bent to pick up her bag, but Gally wriggled out of it. He darted across the floor before she could stop him. He leapt on to Katy's bed and took a swipe at her.

Katy jumped back with a hiss of anger, then tried to bat him away. Gally dodged her hand then took another leap at Katy, but Sophie caught him just in time. She pushed Gally back into the bag. 'I'm sorry,

Katy. I don't know why he's acting like this. He's being really weird.'

'No, he's being just like you – *nasty*!'

'What?' Sophie had never been called nasty before.

Katy reached for her friendship bracelet and pulled it off. She tossed it down on the bed. 'I don't want this any more. It's worthless rubbish.'

Sophie felt breathless, as if she had been slapped. 'Katy,' she said. 'You're my best friend.' She hesitated before she picked up Katy's bracelet and held it out to her. 'Please, let's not fall out.'

Katy looked at the bracelet as if it were a dirty sock. She laughed coldly. '*Friends?* With *you*? I don't think so. Now get out of my room.' She turned her back on Sophie.

Sophie walked to the door. Her heart ached. Surely Katy would turn round. This couldn't be real – it was all too horrible. But Katy didn't turn round.

Trying not to cry, she slowly took off her own friendship bracelet and put them both in her pocket. Sophie turned and went out of the dorm. She'd lost her best friend. And she didn't even understand why.

FOURTEEN

The smell of freshly baking biscuits filled the Food Tech room. Sophie's class was making them for the school's anniversary party. She wished she could look forward to it, but everything was too sad.

She needed the butter on the other side of the counter. Just in front of Katy.

'Pass me the butter, please, Katy?' she said, hoping she would be over the sulk she'd been in for the past two days.

But Katy just ignored her.

Sophie swallowed back tears. *Well, if Katy wants to be horrible, that's her problem,* she told herself. But it wasn't that easy to stop caring.

'Kaz, could you pass me the—' she began.

'So, Erin,' Kaz said loudly, 'are you looking forward to the anniversary party?' She walked away from Sophie without looking at her.

'Yeah,' said Erin. She glanced over her shoulder at Sophie, and Sophie was shocked to see the cold expression in her eyes. She had to be imagining it, right? 'We should get ready together. In the dorms. Like we planned.'

Sophie didn't know what to say. It felt as if her friends were talking about something she wasn't included in. Before she could try and join in the conversation, Abbie caught her eye, reached over and passed her the butter. 'There you go, Sophie,' she said.

Sophie took it with a wobbly smile. 'Thanks, Abbie,' she said.

She looked back at her ingredients. A moment later, she added, 'Oh, I can't remember if Mrs Hepburn said ten or fifteen minutes in the oven. Can you, Lauren?'

Lauren shrugged and moved away.

Sophie couldn't believe it. Then she looked around the kitchen. All her friends except Abbie were bunched up at the end of the work space, as far as they could possibly get from her. She wasn't imagining it. There was definitely something weird going on.

She waited until Mrs Hepburn was on the other side of the room, inspecting the boys' work, and then turned to her friends.

'OK, what's up? What have I done?' she said, trying to force a smile.

She tried to read their faces. Only Abbie looked sympathetic and guilty; the others all scowled at her. Except for Katy, who didn't even look at her as she stirred her biscuit mixture.

'As if you didn't know!' Erin put her arm around Katy's shoulders.

'But I *don't* know!' Sophie said. 'Please tell me. I don't want to fall out—'

'Hi, guys!' Callum, a smudge of flour on his cheek, leaned over the work bench.

'Hi, Callum,' said Sophie, grateful for the distraction.

Abbie waved with a small smile, but the other girls ignored him.

'Um ... Katy, have you ...' Callum started, but tailed off when he saw the expressions of loathing on the girls' faces.

Erin and Kaz looked at each other and rolled their eyes. Lauren flounced round so her back was to him, and Joanna moved off to the far end of the work station. Katy stopped stirring the biscuit mixture, then looked up at Callum, her eyes glaring. 'Go away. I don't want to speak to you ... ever.'

Callum looked as if the air had been knocked out of him. 'What? But why? What have I done?'

'I'm not stupid!' Katy flicked a strand of hair out of her eyes. 'I know what you've been up to with her!'

Sophie found her voice. 'I told you, Katy! Nothing happened with Callum and Abbie ... right, Abbie?'

Katy laughed scornfully. The other girls joined in.

'We know nothing happened with *Abbie*,' Erin said, looking at Sophie with contempt.

'Yeah, she was just a diversion,' Kaz agreed. 'We know it's *you* who snogged Callum!'

147

'What?!' Sophie burst out laughing. 'Me and *Callum*?' The idea was so stupid. 'That's crazy! Callum's like my brother.'

Katy slammed down the spoon. She turned to face Sophie for the first time. Sophie flinched at the look on her face.

'You're such a liar!' she shouted, so that everyone in the room turned to look. 'I know it's true so don't try and deny it.'

'All right, that's it,' Mrs Hepburn snapped, bustling across to them. She clicked her tongue with annoyance and pointed to the door. 'Out! All of you. Don't come back until you can behave like adults.'

Katy ran out of the room, crying. Erin and Kaz followed her, with a last glare at Sophie.

'I don't know how you could be so horrible, Sophie.' Lauren's eyes filled with tears and Joanna put an arm around her shoulders as they turned away.

'But I didn't . . . it's not true—' Sophie began.

'Don't lie! It makes it worse,' Joanna interrupted furiously. She and Lauren followed the others out of the classroom.

Sophie started to cry as she went to the door, Callum and Abbie right behind her.

'It's not true,' she sobbed as soon as they were in the corridor. 'Callum, tell them it's not true. I'd never do anything like that to Katy. I'd never do anything like that to any of my friends!'

Callum looked as miserable as Sophie felt. 'Abbie,' he said, 'Sophie's telling the truth; nothing would ever happen with me and Sophie.'

'I believe you,' Abbie said, putting an arm round both of them. 'I know you wouldn't do that to your friend. And I know you're not the type of guy to cheat on his girlfriend.'

'Thanks, Abbie.' Callum's eyes shone. 'I really appreciate it.'

Abbie smiled and blushed almost as deep a red as her hair. Sophie managed a weak smile. At least she had one friend who trusted her. But something was bothering her even more than the argument.

'I just don't know who can have told them that lie,' she said, drying her eyes. 'Who would start such a mean, cruel rumour in the first place?'

FIFTEEN

Sophie leaned the two folding chairs against the bookshelves in the empty Rare Volumes room of the library. She stood on tiptoes and lifted down the book *Real Physics* from the shelf. She felt a cold draught behind her and looked round to see that the wall had slid open, revealing the long staircase that led down to the magic library. Normally she would have been filled with excitement at helping get ready for a witch party, but she couldn't even muster a smile. Now Katy hated her and all her friends believed a horrible lie about her, neither of the parties was going to be fun at all.

The door to the Rare Volumes room opened. Luckily it was only Callum.

But then Ashton appeared from behind him.

'Hey, guys.' Sophie's heart fluttered a little as she returned Ashton's smile and remembered the moment when they had almost kissed. She quickly looked back at Callum, hoping her blush hadn't been too obvious. 'What's up?'

Ashton and Callum exchanged a glance. Sophie noticed that Ashton looked tense.

'I'm looking for Katy,' he said. 'I thought she might be with Callum, but he told me what happened – that they split up.'

Callum fixed his eyes on the ground.

'I know I wasn't exactly thrilled about you two getting together,' Ashton said to Callum, 'but I've realised I was wrong. You and Katy were great.'

Callum managed a smile.

Ashton turned to Sophie. 'The truth is, I'm worried about Katy. We were supposed to meet to get a call from our parents, but she didn't show up. That's not like her.'

Sophie was shocked. Katy had been so worried about them.

'And then when I *did* speak to my parents, they said all their rituals had prophesied danger at Turlingham!' Ashton's deep green eyes were filled with worry. 'I know that witch hunter magic isn't as powerful as witch magic, so my parents could be wrong, but we need to be careful.'

Sophie smiled, though she didn't feel happy. Ashton was obviously trying really hard to be nice about witches.

'Have you seen Katy?' Callum asked Sophie. 'Could you warn her to be on her guard?'

Sophie sighed. 'I really wish I could ... but she's not talking to me either.'

Ashton raised his eyebrows, but Sophie didn't want to explain why: it would make Katy look bad ... and she didn't want the image of her and Callum kissing in Ashton's head. 'But I do know where she is: she's down in the magic library, helping put up the bunting for the party.'

Ashton looked at the chairs leaning on the book-shelf. 'Were you taking these down?' he asked. 'Can I help?'

He picked up a chair, then put it down again. 'On second thoughts . . . I'd better not. The witches haven't learned to trust me yet.' He gave Sophie a lopsided grin. 'I don't think they'll want me there.'

'Oh, but you—' Sophie began, but Ashton shook his head.

'It's fine. I don't want to make them feel uncom-fortable. Could you just ask Katy to come up? I'll be in one of the practice rooms.'

'Of course,' Sophie said.

Sophie watched the door of the Rare Volumes room close behind him, feeling happier than she had for a long time. Ashton was so different these days. It was almost as if he had become a much nicer person. Maybe he always had been, but just felt he had to hide it. She just wished it didn't feel as if he, Callum and Abbie were the only friends she had left.

Sophie went down the stairs, a chair under each arm. She could hear laughter and conversation echoing along the aisles, and the distant sound of a jazz band. Numbered party lanterns had been strung along the shelves so that people could find their way through the ever-changing library. The strings of lanterns broke off at the end of the aisle and then reappeared in the distance somewhere else. It looked pretty cool, actually. Sophie followed the sound of her dad's voice and came out into a large open space where tables and chairs were being set out. Mrs Clarke and Abbie were standing on chairs, pinning up bunting. Sophie's dad and Mr Clarke were by the food, deep in conversation.

'Andrew, are you blowing up those balloons, or gossiping?' Mrs Clarke called down.

'Sorry, dear!' Mr Clarke hurriedly began pumping the balloons again.

Sophie's dad looked round, saw her and smiled. 'I'll take those chairs,' he said, coming towards her.

'This all looks great!' said Sophie, looking around. 'I thought a witch party would be really different, but everything looks normal. Those are *just* crisps and lemonade, aren't they?'

'Yes.' Her dad laughed. 'Your mother said no magic,

so we're sticking to that. It would be a lot easier if I was allowed to use a spell or two though – the library keeps moving around and we keep losing tables and whatever's on them! I think your grandma is off hunting for a box of party poppers as we speak.'

Sophie laughed. 'And where's Katy?' she asked, looking around.

Her dad frowned. 'I've not seen her recently. She was meant to be helping, but she keeps running off.'

Sophie frowned too. That wasn't like Katy at all.

Her dad raised his voice. 'Anyone seen Katy?'

'I'll find her,' said Abbie hastily. She jumped down from the chair.

'Abbie, no! The bunting!' Mrs Clarke exclaimed as it all fell to the floor. But Abbie had already gone, running off into the aisles. 'Oh, goodness!' She put her hands on her hips. 'There she goes again. Katy's not the only one who keeps going missing.'

Sophie looked up at her dad and made a pleading face. He rolled his eyes and laughed.

'Oh, go on then. You three are clearly up to something!'

Sophie ran off after Abbie into the aisles. *Someone* was up to something – and it wasn't her.

As soon as she was a few steps away, the noise of conversation suddenly disappeared. Sophie turned around. Sure enough, the aisles had moved, and the others were now far away. She could see the glint of the party lanterns in the distance though, and that made her feel brave enough to go on, walking down the corridor of bookshelves.

The tall walls of books towered around her, and there was a hushed, dusty feel to the air. Sophie almost felt as if she ought to go on tiptoe. But as she walked along the aisle she realised she could hear Katy. She was talking to – no, *arguing* with – someone.

She peeked round the corner. Katy and Abbie were in the centre of the aisle. Katy was facing towards Sophie; her fists were clenched and Sophie was shocked at the look of rage on her face.

'Where is it?' Katy demanded.

'I don't know!' Abbie took a step backwards. Katy

moved closer to her, her face just inches from Abbie's.

'You'd better find it.'

'And you'd better do what I say!' Abbie's voice was high and shaking. 'Or else—'

'Or else *what*?' Katy pointed a finger at her. 'If you don't back off I'll tell your parents what you've done. You wouldn't like that, would you?'

'Hey!' Sophie was frightened but determined to find out what was going on. Abbie spun round to face her. Both she and Katy stared at Sophie. Katy looked angry but Abbie was trembling.

Sophie told herself she had nothing to be scared of – they were her friends. But the look on Katy's face gave her the creeps. In the dusky light her eyes almost glowed. Sophie barely recognised her.

'What are you two arguing about?' she said, trying to keep her voice light.

Instead of answering, Katy turned on her heel and stalked off into the shadows.

'Abbie?' Sophie came up to her. 'What happened? Are you OK?'

Abbie wouldn't meet Sophie's eye. 'Nothing. I ...
I'm fine!' She pushed past Sophie and ran back
towards the party lanterns. Sophie was left in the
middle of the aisle, puzzled and confused. Abbie
hadn't looked fine. She had looked absolutely
terrified.

SIXTEEN

Sophie hugged herself, shivering in the frosty air. Over her head, the last leaves of the old oak shivered too. The school towered above her, its turrets lost in the mist.

She checked her phone again. None of her friends had replied to her text asking to meet, and it was five minutes past twelve already. What if they didn't even bother to show up? She felt so alone without them.

The door of the school opened and Sophie gasped with relief as she saw Kaz and Erin coming down the steps towards her, followed by Joanna and Lauren. None of them was smiling – Erin's expression could have cut glass – but at least they'd come.

The girls stopped a little distance away from her. Sophie tried not to show how hurt she felt by their cold faces. This was going to be a hard conversation, but she had to persuade them that the rumour was a lie.

'I'm so glad you came,' she began.

'Well,' said Kaz, 'we almost didn't.'

Lauren looked up at Sophie from under her eyelashes. 'But then we realised we've been friends since Year Seven. We decided to hear you out.'

'Exactly!' said Sophie. 'You know me better than anyone in the world. You know I'd never, ever betray a friend.'

No one answered. Kaz scuffed the ground with her shoe. Erin looked away.

Sophie looked pleadingly at each one in turn. 'Who told you I snogged Callum? Because it's a total lie.'

Still no one answered. Sophie felt tears coming into her eyes.

'Please. I've always been a good friend, haven't I? I don't want to lose you.' Her voice wobbled. She caught Erin's eye and for the first time Erin looked guilty.

Erin and Kaz glanced at each other. Joanna and Lauren looked miserable. Kaz heaved a sigh and said, 'OK, well ... it was Abbie.'

Sophie felt as if the breath had been knocked out of her. *Abbie!* 'How could she?' Sophie muttered. She felt like an idiot for ever trusting her.

There was an embarrassed silence. Erin broke it. 'It's not true, then?'

'I promise!' Sophie said.

'We thought ... ' started Joanna, 'since you've been so close and everything ... that she would be telling the truth about you.'

Sophie gritted her teeth in frustration. 'Abbie's been stealing your boyfriends, breaking up our friendships, and ruining everything at Turlingham. Abbie's made fools of all of us.'

'Oh, Sophie, I'm so sorry we didn't trust you!' Lauren exclaimed. She ran forward to hug Sophie, and the other girls followed at once. Sophie hugged them all back, torn between happiness and anger. How could Abbie have done this to her? And why?

'I'm sorry, Sophie,' Erin said, and the others echoed her. 'Abbie was just so believable.' She sounded genuinely confused. 'Why would she do this?'

'She fooled me too,' said Sophie. She wondered if Abbie had even used magic to influence her friends. 'She's a good liar.'

'I wish she'd never come to Turlingham,' Kaz said angrily.

'Me too.' Erin shook her head.

'I just feel so stupid for telling you all to make friends with her,' Sophie said. 'I just wish there was some way of showing her that she hasn't beaten us ... Wait a minute.' She grinned as an idea hit her. 'What if we played a prank on her to get her back? Nothing nasty, just to show her that she can't split our gang up that easily?'

'That,' said Erin, 'is an amazing idea!'

'Yay!' said Joanna, clapping her hands. 'It's been ages since we had one of Sophie Morrow's world-famous pranks!'

Kaz's eyes went wide and twinkled with wickedness. 'Hey, I know! She likes jokes about dumb blondes . . . how about we swap her shampoo for some blond dye?'

The girls burst out laughing.

'That is the best blonde joke I have ever heard, *ever*!' Erin gave Kaz a high-five. 'Let's do it!'

Sophie raced off with the others to the dorms. Suddenly the whole day seemed warmer and brighter – she had her friends back. The only thing that was missing now was Katy.

'Did you talk to Katy?' she asked hopefully as they ran up the stairs.

Erin shook her head. 'We hardly see her these days. She's acting really weird.'

'Yeah,' Joanna agreed, out of breath as they reached the landing. 'And I don't think it's just because of splitting up with Callum. Since when did she think grey contact lenses were cool?' she added as she pushed open the door to the dorms.

'Grey contact lenses?' Sophie was surprised: Katy had never said anything about wanting grey eyes. But the others were ahead of her and she had to run to catch them up.

'Quiet. Let's see if the coast is clear!' Erin peered into Abbie's dorm. It was empty. 'Kaz, you grab your hair dye. We'll get Abbie's shampoo.'

Kaz scurried off and Sophie went over to Abbie's dressing table. Her pink sponge bag was sitting open on top of it, surrounded by brushes and combs and hairclips. Sophie took a bottle of shampoo from the bag and ran back to the door. She glanced out, beckoned the others after her and ran into the bathroom. A moment later Kaz came in with the dye.

Erin tipped the shampoo down the sink. Kaz carefully poured the dye into the bottle and screwed the top back on.

'Let's see how she likes blonde jokes now!' she said with a grin. Sophie grinned back: Abbie was going to get a shock the next morning.

Sophie kicked off her slippers, jumped on her bed and dialled Callum's number. Jareth Quinn gazed broodingly down at her from her posters, and she tried not to think how much he looked like Ashton. Only, Ashton was better-looking, of course. Her train of thought was broken as Callum picked up and said, 'Hi, Sophie.'

'Hi, Callum. I just wondered if you'd managed to talk to Katy.'

Callum's heavy sigh down the phone told her that he hadn't.

'I just don't get it.' Sophie sighed too. 'She's acting so unlike herself.'

'I know. Why would she believe that we kissed? It makes no sense.'

'Well, I found out who started it!' Sophie quickly told Callum what had happened.

'Abbie? Really?' Callum didn't sound convinced. 'But she's been so nice. There must have been some mistake.'

Sophie shrugged. 'Maybe. I hope so.' She was sure there hadn't been a mistake – she trusted her oldest friends to tell her the truth – but she didn't like the thought of talking about Abbie behind her back. Hopefully she'd learn her lesson when she washed her hair, and that would be the end of it.

'Actually, I've got plans to meet up with Abbie tomorrow.' Callum sounded embarrassed. 'I can ask her then.'

'Callum!' Sophie couldn't believe it. 'You can't still meet her! After what she did to you and me and Katy?' A horrible thought struck Sophie 'It's not *that* kind of meeting up, is it? It's not a d—'

'No!' Callum sounded horrified. 'I'm totally not over Katy – and Abbie wouldn't make a move so soon. She's been really nice to me, Sophie. Really sympathetic. We're just going out as friends.'

Sophie frowned. It all sounded pretty suspicious to her. 'You'd better be careful she's not setting you up for a romance spell,' she told Callum. 'You said she went to the Science lab that day we got rid of Bethan. She could have been finding things for a spell.'

'I can take care of myself,' Callum said.

She really hoped so, because Abbie couldn't be trusted. Callum was clueless about girls, but it was clear to Sophie that Abbie was making a play for him now that Katy was out of the picture.

As she put the phone down she made her mind

up – she couldn't let this go. She'd have to confront Abbie face to face.

The second bell had just rung as Sophie walked along the corridor to Abbie's dorm. Girls ran in and out of the rooms, the noise of hair driers blasting out and squeals of 'We're going to be late!' coming from everywhere. Abbie was nowhere to be seen. The only person who hadn't left for class yet was the girl who had the bed next to Abbie, Claire. She was putting her pencil case and books in her bag.

'Hi, Claire. Have you seen Abbie?' Sophie asked.

'No. She must have got up really early, because she was gone before I woke up.' Claire finished knotting her tie. 'Her bag's there though. See you!' She ran out of the door, leaving Sophie alone in the dorm.

Sophie turned round to look at Abbie's part of the room. Her bed had been roughly made and on it was her schoolbag. It was unzipped and Sophie could see inside. Old pieces of paper, with ragged edges, stuck out of the top.

She stepped forward to have a closer look. The

pages were *really* old. Was Abbie reading up on spells? Something to make Callum fall in love with her, maybe? A few lines caught her eyes: ' … you will know the possessed by their moonstruck eyes … '

A possession spell! But before she read more, she heard footsteps.

Abbie came in, breathless. Her hair was green!

'Abbie!' Sophie gasped. 'Your … your *hair*!'

'It's green!' Abbie shouted. 'And I can guess who's responsible, too!'

'But *how*? I don't understand!' Sophie backed away. She felt really guilty. But this wasn't her fault, was it? They'd dyed her hair blond, not green!

'I got up, washed my hair, went down to the library, and when my hair dried it was green!' Abbie's voice rose higher. '*You* tell *me* how it happened!'

'Abbie, I'm so sorry!' Sophie could see how awful this must be for Abbie. 'We never meant for this to happen. We did put dye in your shampoo. But it was blond. I promise.'

'Blond dye? You mean bleach?' Abbie groaned. 'It must have reacted with my red dye.'

'You mean your hair colour isn't natural?' Sophie was shocked. She had no idea.

'Of course not! No one has hair that colour naturally.' Abbie turned to the mirror, wincing as she stroked her hair. 'This is so embarrassing. I don't know how I'm going to face anyone. The boys are going to—'

'Girls? What's all this noise?' Sophie jumped as her mum walked into the dormitory. 'I could hear you all the way down the corridor. Sophie? What are you doing here? And … *Abbie*?' She stared at Abbie, speechless. 'What on earth happened to your hair?'

'She did it!' Abbie pointed at Sophie.

'Sophie! Did you do this?' Sophie's mum stared at her, and Sophie couldn't deny it. 'After I told you,' she turned to push the door shut, and lowered her voice, '*no magic allowed*!'

'But it wasn't magic!' Sophie exclaimed. 'It was an accident.'

'Don't lie to me.' Her mum raised her eyebrows. 'I'm really angry, Sophie. How could you have done this to a fellow pupil? And disobeyed me like this after you promised!'

Sophie turned to Abbie. 'Abbie, tell her!' she pleaded. 'You know it wasn't magic!'

Instead of answering, Abbie burst into sobs. Sophie's mum put an arm around her.

She looked at Sophie reproachfully. 'I didn't think you were a bully, Sophie. Or a liar.'

'I'm not . . . It wasn't . . . ' Sophie desperately tried to explain, but Abbie just sobbed harder and louder, drowning her out. Sophie's mum hugged Abbie.

'Go to my office at once,' she told Sophie. 'You are in big, big trouble! You're banned from the anniversary party. Both of them!'

Sophie felt a lump in her throat as she walked out of the dorm. And when Abbie looked up and scowled at her so Sophie's mum couldn't see, Sophie was even more cross than ever. Banned from not one but *two* parties!

Abbie was the worst! But she couldn't do much more damage, could she?

SEVENTEEN

Sophie unlocked the back door and stepped out into the dark evening, carefully balancing a bowl of dog food in her hands. Through the hedge she could hear laughter and muffled conversation as people made their way up to the school for the party. Sophie's mouth turned down. She'd been so looking forward to having two parties to go to. Now she had none.

Sophie bent down and put the bowl on the patio next to Mincing's bowl of cat food.

'Rosdet, Mincing,' she called, 'Gally. Come and get

your dinner!' She rattled some nuts in her pocket and looked around for them. She hated that they had to live outside now.

'Dinner! Gally!'

There was a rustle in the grass and Rosdet stepped out of the shadows. Sophie blinked. Callum was right, he really did have purple eyes. They glowed in the light from the back door.

'Where are the other two?' she asked him. But Rosdet just bent his head and started eating.

Sophie tapped her fingers against the door frame, frowning. It was almost as if Mincing and Gally had been keeping their distance since Rosdet arrived. Could they be jealous? Or was there something odd going on? A nasty feeling began to form in the pit of her stomach. Rosdet's eyes were weird. And there were those pages in Abbie's bag – they said the eyes changed when someone was possessed.

She looked at Rosdet, quietly eating his supper. He looked so normal. It was crazy to think that he might have been possessed! Anyway, she reminded herself, from what she had read in the pages, the eyes were meant to be 'moonstruck'. Whatever colour that was, she was willing to bet it was not purple.

But the nagging feeling that there was something wrong with Rosdet would not go away. Her mum had banned her from casting spells. But this was serious. She was sure – *almost* sure – that if her mum knew why she was doing it she would understand. Besides, how much more trouble could she possibly get into?

She pushed open the door.

'It's cold out here, Rosdet,' she said. 'Why not go inside and get warm by the fire?'

Rosdet shook his tail and his ears and jumped nimbly over the doorstep. He trotted into the house.

Sophie picked up the key from the windowsill, shut the door behind her and set off up the path to her dad's shed. She felt a bit bad about tricking Rosdet, but if it turned out to be a false alarm at least he would have had a cosy evening.

Sophie unlocked the door of the shed and pushed it open. The shed was warm and had a comfortable smell that reminded Sophie of her dad. Bunches of herbs hung from the rafters, and she ducked among them and switched on the desk lamp. Angelica's chair was empty. Grandma had even taken her aunt to the party. She tried not to feel too sorry for herself.

The door creaked open, Gally pushing it with his nose.

'Gally!' Sophie cried. 'Have you come to help?' He jumped up on her shoulder and nuzzled her cheek. 'Come on then,' she said to him, 'there's work to be done.'

Light glinted from the brass model of a fox that her dad kept on his bookshelf. The fox propped up several very old books, their covers long gone, the pages yellow and curling and threads escaping from the binding. Sophie took down the closest one and turned to the index, scanning down the Ps for 'Possession'. There was nothing in that book or the next one. But in the third book:

'Possession!' Sophie exclaimed. She sat down in Angelica's chair and, rocking absent-mindedly, began to read.

'Mugwort,' she said to herself. 'I'm sure I've seen a bottle of that in here somewhere. Mint – I can get that

from the kitchen. Ivy – got loads of that in the garden.'
Sophie jumped to her feet and began looking through
her dad's rack of herbs. She lined them up on the desk
and then went outside to pick the rest of the plants.
Shivering in the cold air, she ran back to the house.
She glanced into the living room. Rosdet was curled in
front of the fire, nose under his tail. He opened an eye
sleepily as Sophie slipped out to the kitchen.

In the kitchen, she followed the recipe, pounding
the herbs up in a pestle and mortar.

'I think I've got it right,' she said to Gally, taking a
sniff. The smell that came from the mixture made her
feel quite dizzy.

There was just one more thing she needed: a compass. Sophie hurried upstairs and got her Geography
one. Mr Powell would never believe what she was
using it for!

She carried the mixture into the sitting room and
sat down by Rosdet. She put the compass in front of
her. She couldn't touch it or the magnet inside would
mean her powers wouldn't work. The needle wobbled
and pointed to north.

'Powers of the Earth,' she said, tossing a pinch of the mixture into the air. As she named each of the four great forces she tossed a pinch to each of the four compass directions. She remembered how Abbie had said her spells in rhyme. Maybe she should try that, she thought. She cleared her throat. 'If someone's here who shouldn't be, bring them out – set Rosdet free.'

Rosdet growled and leapt to his feet. His hackles rose and he snarled at her with white teeth. Startled, Sophie jerked backwards. A purple vapour was rising from the fox, as if he was steaming. Sophie gasped, frightened that she had hurt him somehow. But as she watched, she saw a face forming in the purple vapour. It was a man – balding, but with some ginger hair and wearing spectacles. Sophie knew him.

'R . . . R . . . Robert?' she stammered.

Robert Lloyd cackled. 'Ha! So you finally got it, did you? Took you long enough. My aura was right there, shining in this stupid fox's eyes for you all to see, but even the great Franklin Poulter was too blind to spot it.'

Robert Lloyd was Katy's uncle, a witch hunter, who

had been married to Angelica. He'd watched as Sophie demagicked her, and then he ran to save himself.

'What are you doing to Rosdet?' Sophie clenched her fists.

The face was spiralling into the air, and Sophie realised the draught was drawing it towards the fire. 'Your poor naïve father – so anxious to get his fox back he listened to the magical message I sent, never questioning who sent it. I've seen everything through Rosdet's eyes. And I have plans ... ' He flashed a grin at Sophie.

Sophie was worried. He looked as wild and mad as Angelica did at her worst. 'Have you come for my aunt?' she asked.

'Stupid little witch!' He laughed again. 'My plans are much bigger than that. The biggest. I want power,' he growled, 'and revenge.' And with a last cruel cackle the witch hunter whooshed up the chimney. The fire coughed out purple sparks. Rosdet swayed. Sophie was just in time to catch him before he hit the floor.

'Rosdet!' She laid him down gently on the hearth

rug. The fox's eyelids fluttered. When he opened them his eyes weren't purple any longer. He gazed at Sophie with grateful, loving kindness.

Sophie stroked Rosdet's head, trying to calm herself as much as him.

'You poor thing!' Sophie felt so stupid for being tricked like this.

There was a sound of small claws scraping at the door. Sophie got up and opened it. Gally dashed in, followed by Mincing. They raced up to Rosdet and snuggled up to him. Mincing purred, Gally stroked Rosdet's ears and Rosdet thumped his tail weakly.

'You knew there was something wrong the whole time, didn't you?' Sophie patted Gally's head. 'I'm sorry I didn't understand.'

Sophie went outside and fetched Rosdet's food bowl and his water. So Robert had been possessing him, spying on them the whole time for some sort of evil plan. That was bad. *Really* bad. She was angry with herself for not noticing sooner. She should have wondered earlier about the purple eyes. She recalled the notes in Abbie's bag – only the eyes were meant to be 'moonstruck', weren't they? And moonstruck wasn't purple. If she had to guess, she'd say it was ...

She dropped the bowl. It clattered on the floor, food spilling out.

'Katy's eyes!' she gasped. Katy hadn't been wearing grey contact lenses. They were silver. Silver as *moonlight*. Katy was possessed too!

Sophie turned and ran out of the room, leaving the bowl where it had landed. She tugged on her boots, almost tripping over her feet in her haste. Everything began to fall into place – Katy had started acting weirdly as soon as Bethan's spirit disappeared. Bethan must have possessed Katy, and her silver witch's aura was making her eyes look silver! But how had it happened? Was it something she and Ashton had done? Pulling on her coat as she went, she ran out of the front door and down the path towards the school. It didn't matter that she was grounded – she had to find Katy at once, and drive Bethan's spirit out of her before it did her serious harm.

As Sophie ran along the path she could hear music coming from the Turlingham party. In the courtyard the trees were decked with fairy lights. The windows blazed with light and the doors stood wide open. Sophie glimpsed the school Christmas tree, put up for the first time that year and decked in gold and silver. People stood on the lawn, clutching glasses and plates, laughing and talking happily. Behind them she could hear the sound of the school orchestra playing carols.

Sophie slowed, out of breath, as she reached the main doors. She pushed her way up the stairs, through the crowd, following the sound of the orchestra.

'Excuse me. Sorry.' She ducked under the elbow of a tall man in a suit and found herself face to face with Abbie, just inside the door. The look on Abbie's face brought her up short. Her face was white and tears spilled from her eyes.

'Abbie?' she said, shocked. 'What's the matter?'

'Oh, Sophie,' Abbie sobbed. 'I've done something terrible. And now I think the whole school is in danger!'

Sophie steered her out of the crowd into the shelter of the Christmas tree.

'Calm down. Whatever's happened, it can't be that

bad.' She glanced over her shoulder, looking for Katy in the crowd.

'It's worse! It's ... it's Katy.'

'What?' Sophie whipped back round to face Abbie. 'What's happened to Katy?'

Abbie hung her head, tears rolling from her eyes. 'It was me who stole the pages from the spell book,' she whispered. 'I didn't want Bethan's soul to be at peace. I wanted to use her ghost to get what I wanted!'

Sophie stared at her in horror.

'I just wanted Callum to fancy me,' Abbie sobbed. 'He was so into Katy and there was no way I'd ever have a chance with him unless they split up. So I did a ritual.' Abbie couldn't look at Sophie. 'To make Bethan's spirit possess Katy.'

'Oh, Abbie!' Sophie was furious, and frightened too. But something that had been puzzling her finally made sense. 'So when me and Ashton did our ritual and it seemed to work ...'

'Bethan's spirit hadn't gone away. I did it. I made Bethan go into Katy.' Abbie nodded. She caught Sophie's eye. 'I know it was stupid. I didn't mean it to get out of hand. It was OK at first: she did what I wanted to and, while she was inside Katy, she broke up with Callum.'

'I bet she did,' said Sophie grimly. Bethan hated the Gibsons so much, she would have been happy to ruin Katy's relationship.

'But after that, she stopped listening to me. She just laughed when I tried to tell her what to do. I'm scared, Sophie.'

'But why don't you just use the spell from the book to put her spirit to rest?' Sophie demanded. 'I saw it in your bag—'

'Those are just the pages about possession. I hid the last page, the one with the spell for putting her to rest, in the library.' Abbie began to sob again. 'And n-now the library's ch-changed . . .'

' . . . and you can't find it,' Sophie finished for her.

'I've looked for it everywhere. That's what I was looking for when you interrupted me arguing with Katy – I mean, Bethan. I'm so frightened, Sophie. Bethan's out of control. I never meant for this to happen!'

'Abbie, calm down,' Sophie interrupted. There was no time to panic, and no time for her to be angry with Abbie. They had to do something. 'We'll just have to work together to find the spell before Bethan makes Katy do something really bad.'

Sophie raced up the corridor towards the library, Abbie sniffling behind her. Sophie skidded round a corner, and stopped in surprise. Ashton was leaning against the wall. He was clutching his nose and blood was dripping through his fingers.

'Ashton!' She gazed at him in horror, then ran up to him. 'Are you OK?'

Ashton took his hand away for long enough to say, in a muffled voice, 'Katy. She's gone crazy!'

'Oh no.' Sophie exchanged a glance with Abbie.

'I saw her going to the library. She had a candle and a can of lighter fluid. I asked her what she was doing and she . . . she just pushed me.' Ashton sounded as if he still couldn't believe it. 'She said she wanted to burn down the magical library so no one can ever get rid of her.' He swallowed and went on: 'I tried to stop her, and she punched me in the nose!' He shook his head in disbelief, scattering drops of blood. 'Her eyes ... they were really strange ...'

Sophie's mouth felt dry and she realised she was shaking.

'She's not crazy, she's possessed,' she said.

Ashton looked at her in horror. 'Possessed?' He tried to move but Sophie pushed him back against the wall.

'Not you. You're hurt,' she told him. She knew she had to think fast; there was no time for mistakes.

'But—'

'Find my mum. Tell her what's going on. Me and Abbie will handle this.'

'I can't let you go alone.' He grabbed her wrist as she turned away.

'The witches will panic if they see you rush in,' Abbie spoke up. She was pale but her voice was firm, and Sophie knew she was right. 'If they see a witch hunter crash their party ... there could be trouble.'

Ashton hesitated. Sophie could see he was struggling to decide what to do.

'Abbie's right.' She gently took his hand from her

wrist. 'We'll be fine, Ashton.' She smiled at him, hoping he couldn't see how scared she was. 'Come on, Abbie!' She was already running, Abbie behind her, towards the library. They had to stop Katy *now* before she killed the witches in the library and the humans at the party above them.

EIGHTEEN

Sophie raced down the corridor, Abbie right behind her. She skidded across the flagstones and pushed open the door of the library. The bookshelves loomed darkly around them as they ran to the Rare Volumes room. Sophie snatched *Real Physics* off the shelf, and as soon as the secret door yawned open she ran down the stairs.

The witches had lined the steps with lanterns, and as she reached the bottom Sophie could hear the sound of distant music, squeals of laughter and happy conversation echoing down the aisles of books.

'Come on! This way.' She led Abbie through the aisles, following the lanterns. As they drew closer to the party, the sounds died away and Sophie heard a single voice speaking. It was her grandma, and she was making a speech.

'. . . so much has changed in the three hundred years since Benedict Wapentake established this library.' Sophie rounded a corner and stopped in the shadow of the aisle. In front of her, all the witches were listening to her grandma, cradling their glasses and plates. 'What may the next three hundred years bring?'

Sophie looked through the crowd. Her dad stood with Mr Clarke, an attentive frown on his face, nodding along as his mother spoke.

'I can't see her anywhere,' Abbie whispered breathlessly behind her.

'Let's not disturb them,' Sophie said in a low voice. 'If we find Katy before she does anything, they'll never need to know.' If the witches found Katy there might be trouble – she was a witch hunter, after all.

They hurried along the aisles, looking this way and

that. At the end of the next aisle, Abbie stopped and sniffed. A frightened look came over her face.

'I can smell ... I think I can smell ...'

Smoke! Sophie smelled it too.

She broke into a run. As they went down the aisle the smell of smoke became stronger, and in a moment she could hear the crackle of flames. Sophie felt sick. They were too late. Then she saw a red glow leaping across the shelves, and a dark figure standing silhouetted in front of it. The figure turned round, and hissed as she saw them. It was Katy – and her eyes were silver as the moon.

Barely stopping to think, Sophie stretched out a hand.

'Earth, water, wind and fire – stop her!'

She hadn't even been sure what the spell would do, but to her shock an orb of white energy burst from the tips of her fingers and knocked the candle out of Katy's hands. The candle went out as it fell, and rolled away into the shadows.

'Bethan, stop!' Abbie cried. 'There are people in the library. Witches, the same as us! You'll hurt them.'

Katy grinned. She lifted her hands in a sudden

movement like a bird taking flight. A gust of wind blew down the aisle, whipping Sophie's hair and clothes, and fanned the burning books. The flames spat silver sparks and with a gleeful whoosh the fire leapt to the next shelf.

'Hurt? I don't care who I hurt. Why should I?' Katy cackled. She waved a hand again and the fire clambered up the shelves as if it were climbing a ladder. 'I'm not going anywhere.'

'Bethan, please, no!' Sophie flinched as smouldering paper fell around her.

Katy ignored her. She turned in a circle, her grinning face lit by firelight.

'It's going to be such fun to live again, in this pretty young body!' she announced. 'I couldn't have chosen a better vessel if I'd tried. Thank you, Abbie, you silly little fool!'

She turned and strode deeper into the library. Sophie exchanged a horrified glance with Abbie.

Raising her voice to be heard over the flames, she said: 'We've got to put our powers together. We've got to get Bethan out of Katy!'

'But how?' Abbie sounded as if she were about to cry.

Sophie felt in her pocket and pulled out the herbs and the compass she had used on Rosdet.

'I think this spell will work,' she said, the sweat running down her face as the heat grew stronger. 'If we're strong enough. Together.'

Abbie's voice trembled as she said, 'We might be strong enough, but I don't know if I'm brave enough.'

Sophie reached out and gripped her hand. 'We've *got* to be brave enough. Come on!'

As Sophie ran down the aisles after Katy, she felt heat rolling out from the burning books to each side. Her palms were sweating with fear but she knew they couldn't turn back. Up ahead in the shadows she could hear Katy still talking and cackling to herself.

'Yes, and in the body of a witch hunter too! Such fun! Such a chance for revenge!'

Revenge! There was that word again.

'Here, take these.' Sophie stopped and poured some herbs into Abbie's cupped hands. She hoped what she was about to do would work. It was a risk, but there was nothing else to try. 'Copy me.'

Sophie tossed the herbs to the four compass points and Abbie did the same.

'Earth, water, wind and fire,' Sophie began. She locked gazes with Abbie. Slowly, so Abbie could echo her, she said: 'Someone's here who shouldn't be. Bring them out. Set Katy free!'

She took Abbie's hands in her own, and they stood facing each other, repeating the spell over and over again. Sophie hoped as hard as she could that they would be a strong enough circle.

'Someone's here who shouldn't be. Bring them out. Set Katy free!'

'Set Katy free!' Abbie repeated. Sophie could see the terror in her eyes.

There was a distant, furious scream. Sophie looked up to see Bethan's ghost seeping out of Katy like steam. Then it rushed at them down the aisle, tearing flaming books from the shelves as she went. Just in time, Sophie ducked to one side, and Abbie to the other. But to Sophie's horror a huge, iron-bound book hit Abbie right on the temple. She fell to the ground, sprawled motionless.

Sophie got to her feet. Bethan wasn't coming back for her – she was heading for the party!

Katy was lying on the ground ahead. As Sophie watched, she groaned and pushed herself up, her head drooping.

'Katy!' Sophie rushed to her and helped her to her feet.

'Sophie!' Katy was sobbing. 'I'm sorry! It was like I was trapped in my own body ... and I couldn't do anything ... All those things I said – she said. I—'

'We've no time, we've got to stop her!' Sophie helped Katy along the corridor to where Abbie was lying. 'If she reaches the party she might possess someone else. And the fire – it's spreading.'

'Oh, she won't possess anyone else!' Katy's voice was stronger now, and fierce. 'I'll see to that!' She opened her schoolbag. 'I know I've got some pearls in here – and mercury – and I can make hydrochloric acid ...'

She shook the contents on to the ground.

'Hurry, Katy!' Sophie could hear wailing in the

distance. Bethan flew back towards them. Katy tossed the ingredients directly into the burning books. The fire crackled and spat and changed colour into a rainbow. Black clouds boiled from it.

'Noooooo!' Bethan screamed. She spun round and round, drilling through the air. Sophie tried to shield Katy as heavy books pummelled them.

'*Continens pro quod continentur. Incarcerare! Incarcerare!*' Katy flung the last ingredient, a pearl, into the flames.

Bethan screamed. She hung in the air, seemingly frozen.

'I forgot a container!' Katy looked around, an expression of panic on her face.

Sophie tried to think. There was nothing here to put Bethan into, except ... She grabbed a book and held it out to Katy.

'A book?' Katy asked. 'How is that a container?'

'Contains writing.' Sophie grinned. Katy grinned back and opened the book.

'*Incarcerare! Incarcerare!*' she chanted.

Bethan screamed. The sound sliced through the air

and Sophie covered her ears as she heard the pain in it.

'No! I don't want to go back! I don't want to go back! I don't want to go baaaaaaaaaa ...'

As Bethan screamed she seemed to stretch out of the air, down towards the book. Sophie held her breath as Bethan was slowly drawn into the paper. Katy's spell was working in a way that Ashton's had not. Bethan's image finally appeared on the page, writhing and wriggling, a furious woman with a snake twisted around her, binding her, its jaws open in a hiss.

Then Katy slammed the book shut.

Katy let out a long, shuddering breath of relief. Sophie had tears in her eyes. What they had done felt so cruel, but she knew they had no choice. She pulled herself together and looked at Katy.

'The fire. We've got to get everyone out!'

NINETEEN

Sophie staggered along the aisles as fast as she could, but it wasn't easy with Abbie leaning on her shoulder, wobbly from being hit on the head. Katy followed them. Sophie could see she was still exhausted from the possession. She tried not to panic – but they were a long way from the witches, and if Katy collapsed too ...

She gasped in relief as she finally heard the noise of the party. She turned the corner of the aisle and saw the witches milling about, laughing and eating.

Her dad and the Clarkes were talking over the music, her dad with a lopsided party hat and Mr Clarke balancing a plate of nibbles. She used the last of her strength to break into a run, dragging Abbie along. It felt as if they would never reach the end of the aisle.

'Help! Help us!' she shouted. Her voice was hoarse from the smoke, and no one heard. It was like shouting in a nightmare. Sophie forced her voice louder. 'HELP! FIRE!'

Her dad turned in surprise, and the witches looked around as Sophie, Katy and Abbie staggered into the party. Sophie's knees buckled, and her dad leapt to support her. Mr Clarke caught Abbie just in time.

'What? That's the witch hunter girl!' A tall witch with a wolverine curled around her shoulders pointed at Katy. Sophie heard gasps and people turned sharply to stare. Some witches murmured threateningly.

Katy swallowed and looked nervous. She clutched the book containing Bethan to her chest.

Sophie's dad ignored the witches. He looked at his daughter. 'Sophie, what did you say?'

Sophie gulped air into her smoke-roughened throat and whispered, 'Fire.'

Her dad's eyes opened wide.

'We've got to hurry,' she said.

A chorus of shocked murmurs broke out. Mrs Clarke sniffed the air, her nose twitching.

Sophie's grandma's voice was calm but firm as she said: 'Quick, everyone – we need rain spells, *now!*'

The witches leapt into action. Some delved in their pockets for herbs, others raised their arms and began chanting. A few joined hands and formed a circle. Sophie heard the muttering and shouting of magic words all around her, like gathering thunder. But would they be fast enough to beat the fire? It was racing down the aisles towards them, and she could feel the building heat.

Just in time, there was a rumble and heavy rain burst over them. The water soaked Sophie instantly, but she didn't care. The heat died away and thick black smoke filled the aisles. Sophie coughed and choked and shivered in her wet clothes, covering her mouth and nose against the smoke.

A sharp gust of wind blew through the aisles, and the smoke cleared. Sophie saw her grandma, unable to help as she'd been demagicked, but watching all the witches at work.

'We've got to get out of here. Follow the lanterns – all of you, quickly!'

Sophie held back as her dad tried to push her towards the stairs.

'No, we can't go – we need the spell to put Bethan at peace. Otherwise she'll be trapped in that book for ever.'

'Where is the spell?' Sophie's dad looked around, the witches pouring past them towards the exit.

'Abbie knows. Abbie!' Sophie made her way over to Abbie, who was leaning on her mum's shoulder. She was awake but looking dazed. 'Abbie, what aisle number did you put the spell in?' She shook Abbie gently. 'It's important!'

'Aisle two hundred and three,' Abbie managed at last. 'But I told you . . . it moved.'

'We can find it,' Sophie's dad broke in. He reached into his top pocket and pulled out a map of the library. The shelf numbers wriggled around the page, but before Sophie could find aisle 203, flames began to burn up the paper in spots. Sophie guessed that these were the places the fire had broken out. Her dad yelped as the fire touched his fingers. He dropped the paper. It crumpled in flame and reached the floor as smouldering ashes.

'Plan B,' he said grimly. He took off his pocket watch and held it on the palm of his hand. He muttered a few words over it and the hands spun as if they were on a compass. The long hand wavered and ended up pointing away from him, down one of the smoky aisles.

'This way!' He broke into a run, following the trembling watch hand. Sophie ran after him.

Smoke filled the aisles. Sophie put a hand over her nose and mouth, trying not to breathe it in. She could hardly see her dad, even though she could hear him muttering spells just ahead of her.

'It's here, close by.' Sophie's dad's voice was hoarse. He began to chant, 'Powers of the Earth: water, earth, wind and fire, bring the spell I seek to me!' He gestured with his hands, as if he were summoning the air towards him. 'Powers of the—' He broke down, coughing from the smoke and doubling over. Sophie could see he wouldn't be able to finish the spell. She grabbed his hands, forming a circle.

'Powers of the Earth,' she gasped, her eyes watering. 'Earth, water, wind and fire – bring us the spell we seek.' She hoped it would be enough. And it was. A breath of wind parted the clouds of smoke and a shaft of light broke through. Along the light, towards them, floated a single page with a ripped edge.

Sophie grabbed it and read the first line: *To give the restless rest.*

'That's it, Dad!' She clutched the paper tight. 'Let's get out of here.'

They stumbled through the aisles towards the exit, following the distant sound of the fire alarm. Sophie's head was spinning and she was hardly able to keep going. It was just her dad's support that helped her up the stairs and into the school library. Even there, it was smoky. The fire alarm was ringing so loudly that they couldn't speak. They struggled out of the library, down the deserted stairs and through the main doors of the school into the cold, fresh air of the panic-stricken courtyard.

Sophie ran her hands over her face, stunned by the sudden cold and the noise all around them. Everyone was in the courtyard, two ambulances were parked by the gates and people were milling back and forth in confusion. Mrs Freeman rushed past with a register. Sophie had never seen her look frightened before. Maggie Millar was shepherding scared-looking Year 7s away from the school. Sophie saw Abbie, wrapped in a blanket, with her parents close by her.

'Katy!' she exclaimed as the crowd parted and she glimpsed her friend sitting on the ground, her face white. Forgetting her own exhaustion, she ran towards her – but the wolverine witch got there first. Sophie sucked in a gasp as the witch bent down … but the woman wrapped her own coat around Katy. Sophie breathed out and smiled as she heard her say, 'Are you all right, dear? Keep calm now, the ambulance will get to you in a moment.'

Sophie wriggled through the crowd towards Katy as

the wail of the fire engine's siren drew nearer. She realised that quite a few of the people offering help were witches, and although they were bringing coats and making way for the ambulance crews, her witch hearing could pick up a number of healing spells being whispered.

She reached Katy and gave her a hug. 'Katy, are you OK?'

Katy looked shaken but she hugged her back. 'Oh, Sophie, it was horrible,' she said. 'I'm so sorry for—'

'Shhh,' Sophie soothed her, stroking her hair. 'I know it wasn't you.'

'Sophie! Katy!' Sophie looked up to see Erin, looking terrified, pushing through the crowd towards them, followed by Joanna and Lauren. Erin flung her arms around Sophie and Katy and hugged them both tightly. 'Oh my gosh, I'm so glad you're safe.'

'Me too!' Joanna joined the hug, and Lauren bundled in too. 'I couldn't see you anywhere when Mrs Freeman was taking the register, I was so scared!'

Sophie hugged all her friends tightly. They might fall out now and then, but it was like having a hot-water bottle in her heart to know that they really cared for each other.

'Hey, Katy!' Kaz came running through the crowd, shouldering past the other boys and girls. She sounded breathless and looked frightened. 'I just saw your brother. He ran into the building before I could stop him.' She looked back and forth between Katy and Sophie. 'He said he was going into the library to look for you—'

Sophie didn't hear the rest of her sentence. She was running towards the school building, as fast as she could.

TWENTY

'Sophie! Sophie!' Sophie's arm was grabbed from behind and she jerked to a halt, turning to see Katy holding her back. Katy looked terrified, but she said, 'Don't go, Sophie, it's too dangerous. The fire brigade will get him.'

Sophie shook her head. 'They don't know about the secret library!'

She pulled away from Katy's grasp and ran towards the school, ducking and weaving through the crowd. Her heart hammered as she raced up the steps.

Her mind was full of horrible images: Ashton unconscious on the floor, Ashton trapped by flames, Ashton clutching his throat as the smoke suffocated him. She swung round the corner, raced down the corridor and burst through the doors of the library. The fire alarm was still screaming and it was pitch dark in the library, with only the green emergency lighting marking the way to the Rare Volumes room. Unable to see *Real Physics* in the smoky darkness, Sophie pulled all the books off the shelf. They crashed to the floor and the door to the secret library sighed open. Sophie reeled back, putting her sleeve to her nose and mouth as smoke gushed out.

'Earth, water, air and fire – clear my way,' she gasped.

There was a gust of wind and the smoke cleared enough for Sophie to see where she was going. She gathered all her courage and ran down the stairs. Ashton needed her.

Using the wind spell to push away the smoke clouds in front of her, Sophie felt her way through the aisles. She felt panic rising inside her like a fire fanned by the breeze. She was sweating with the effort of keeping the wind spell going and it was so dark that she couldn't see her way. Holding on to the shelves to guide herself along, she edged through the library.

'Ashton!' she screamed.

There was no reply, just the dull crackle of books smouldering, and the drip-drip of water left over from the rain spell. Sophie felt hopeless. And then she remembered – she could use her witch hearing to find Ashton.

She concentrated harder than she had ever concentrated before. The layers of noise seemed to peel away until she found a small, distant sound: the sound she had been hoping for.

Thud-thud. Thud-thud.

A heartbeat. Ashton was still alive!

'I'm coming, Ashton!' she shouted.

She felt her way through the library, following the sound. She jumped as a shelf of books, charred beyond rescue, collapsed next to her. As the crashing died away she realised that the heartbeat was just on the other side of the fallen shelf.

She got on to her hands and knees, clambering over the wreckage. The heartbeat was closer ... and closer ... and then her hand touched something soft and warm. It was Ashton's face. She couldn't hear him breathing.

Sophie felt desperately for a pulse. His heart was beating, but it was as weak as a mouse's. Sophie found out why in a second. The shelf had collapsed on his legs. He was trapped, and unconscious.

If Ashton died ...

'Ashton, wake up!' she screamed, shaking him. He couldn't be dead. He couldn't. She wouldn't let him be. She lifted his head and pressed her lips to his. She couldn't remember how to do the kiss of life – but it didn't seem to matter. Ashton shuddered deeply, then took a gulp of air. Sophie sobbed aloud as he began breathing again.

'Come on, Ashton. Lean on me.' Ashton groaned, and managed to stand up. She helped him out from under the wreckage, steadying herself on the book-shelves as they walked. 'That's right – we'll soon be out of here.' Step by step, fighting against the smoke that pressed down on them, she managed to get Ashton to the exit. He collapsed on the bottom step. Sophie shook his shoulders.

'Ashton, come on. You can't give up now!'

Half walking, half crawling, they made their way up the stairs. Sophie hauled Ashton out of the Rare Volumes room and he slumped to the ground. Sophie collapsed next to him. She was so tired that she couldn't even think. She realised dimly that the fire alarm wasn't sounding any more ...

And then she was outside, and the cold air was like an icy shower.

She opened her eyes. She was lying on a stretcher. Around her, firemen and ambulance crews were working. A man in a high-visibility jacket came towards her. Sophie struggled to prop herself up.

'Ashton ...' she gasped, but she didn't have the strength to say any more.

She felt herself being lifted into the ambulance. She turned to her side and saw Ashton lying on a stretcher next to her. Her heart felt warm as she saw him smiling weakly at her. Even with his face covered in soot and a trickle of dried blood, he was still the most gorgeous boy she'd ever seen.

She cleared her throat. 'Hey, Ashton,' she whispered. The ambulance doors closed and she felt the engine start up. She reached across to him and took his hand. 'I've been thinking about what you said before and ... I'd love to go out with you. If you still want me to, that is.'

She held her breath. Ashton was silent for a second, then he smiled. His green eyes shone as he answered, hoarsely, 'I've been waiting a long time to hear you say that, Sophie.'

Sophie felt a huge smile breaking over her face as she closed her eyes.

Sophie looked out of the window as her dad stopped their car in front of Abbie's house. It was a sunny day and the golden light made the frost on the trees shine even brighter. Abbie's newly re-dyed auburn hair glinted as she came out of her house, carrying a box piled high with books and clothes. She saw Sophie, and hitched the box to one side to wave.

Sophie glanced at Katy, who was sitting next to her on the back seat. Katy looked much better than she had a week ago. The deep shadows under her eyes were almost gone and a few healed scratches on her cheeks were the only evidence of the danger she had been through.

They got out of the car and followed Sophie's parents up to the house.

Mr Clarke, carrying a roll of brown tape, came out of the front room. Sophie's dad looked around at the boxes stacked high.

'We're so sorry you're moving,' he said.

Mrs Clarke put down the vase she was holding. 'We came to release our ancestor's spirit, and now that's done we're moving on.'

Sophie's dad nodded. 'Despite all the ... trouble, it has been a pleasure to have another witch family nearby.'

'I'm sorry too,' said Mrs Clarke. She looked at Sophie's mum. 'And I'm particularly sorry to have brought Abbie here under false pretences. I hope you understand why we did it.'

'I do,' said Sophie's mum. She glanced at Sophie and at her husband. 'I know how important family is.'

Katy coughed shyly and turned to Mr Clarke. 'These are yours,' she said.

She opened her schoolbag and took out a piece of paper and a book. Sophie saw at once that the piece of paper was the spell to put Bethan's spirit to peace. And the book ... well, it was ancient-looking, with a golden image of a hissing snake on its leather cover. She shivered as she thought of Bethan hissing inside.

Mr Clarke took them both. 'Thank you so much,' he said to Katy. 'You needn't worry about Bethan ever again. We will put her unhappy spirit to rest.'

'This wipes out the grudge between your family and ours,' Mrs Clarke joined in. 'The spell your ancestor cast to hurt, you have cast to heal. We are very grateful to you, Katy Gibson.'

Katy blushed. Mrs Clarke reached out to shake her hand – then seemed to change her mind. She pulled Katy into a motherly hug. This time Katy's smile was huge and real.

Abbie touched Sophie on the arm and drew her to one side.

'I'm sorry,' she said, looking into Sophie's eyes. 'I know I've behaved pretty badly in a lot of ways. The thing is … well, I've always used magic to get people to like me.' She blushed and looked down. 'I suppose I didn't really think they'd like me otherwise.'

'Of course they'll like you, if you just show them the real you.'

Abbie smiled, her blue eyes dancing. 'You forgive me then?'

Sophie smiled back warmly. 'Absolutely!'

As they walked back to the car, Sophie could see Katy's friendship bracelet on her wrist again, the gold daisy twinkling as it caught the light. She was wearing hers too, and she felt happier than she had done all term. Everything was back to normal – she and Katy were BFFs again. Only one thing had changed: she had a wonderful, gorgeous boyfriend!

EPILOGUE

Sophie ran down the corridor, dodging the crowds of students who were coming out of their classes. The walls were covered in Christmas decorations and boughs of holly were pinned up over the classroom doors. She clutched an envelope in her hand.

'Erin!' she called, spotting Erin's blond ponytail ahead of her, next to Kaz. Erin turned. 'Have you seen Ashton – I mean, Katy and Ashton?' she asked, blushing and breathless.

'No, not for a while.' Erin glanced at her envelope. 'Is that Katy's card?'

'Oh, um ...' Sophie was relieved that a second later Joanna and Lauren came rushing up, and she didn't have to reply. She ran down the corridor towards the boys' dorms. She couldn't wait to give Ashton his card; she'd made it herself. Her heart hopped, skipped and jumped. Would he have a card for her?

She peeked through the door of the boys' common room, but Ashton wasn't in there. She ran back down to the library, but that was still shut for refurbishing work after the fire. She even tried the classrooms, but they were empty – the students couldn't have left fast enough, seeing as it was the last lesson of term. The corridors seemed to echo as if the holidays had already begun.

Sophie, feeling more and more puzzled, went out of the school and into the courtyard. The sun was setting, casting a red glow over the stone flags, and turning the last leaves on the trees to flames. She looked around. Groups of boys and girls were talking and laughing together, some with their suitcases already packed and ready for their lifts. Mr McGowan was standing near the gate saying goodbye to some of the students. Sophie walked over to him.

'Mr McGowan,' she said, 'have you seen Ashton or Katy anywhere?'

Mr McGowan turned to her and smiled.

'The Gibsons? You've missed them, I'm afraid. They've already left.'

Sophie stood staring at him with her mouth open. *Left?* Without telling her? Without even saying goodbye? Or Happy Christmas?

'So early?' she managed finally. The card in her hand drooped. She knew she hadn't been allowed to know where they were spending the holiday, just in case, but couldn't the Gibsons have let their children say goodbye? Ashton hadn't even bothered to stick around and wait for five minutes.

Mr McGowan nodded, looking at her sympathetically.

'There must have been a change of plan. Their uncle came to pick them up—'

'Uncle?' asked Sophie. A sick feeling of dread rose inside her.

'Yes,' he replied, 'their Uncle Robert.'

Sophie's breath came fast and she hardly heard Mr McGowan's words.

'Sophie? Sophie, are you OK?'

Katy and Ashton only had one Uncle Robert, and the last time she'd seen *him* he'd sworn revenge. Just what was he planning to do to them? They had to be rescued!

Want more magic, mystery
and mayhem?

The Witch of Turlingham Academy
continues in:
Spellbound